Billy Bobble
Makes a Magic Wand

Cubs Rock!

Billy Bobble Makes a Magic Wand

BY R.S. MELLETTE

Billy Bobble Makes a Magic Wand

Copyright © R.S. Mellette 2014

All rights reserved.
No part of this book may be used or reproduced in any manner whatsoever without permission, except in the case of brief quotations embodied in critical articles and reviews.

Book Design: R.C. Lewis
Illustrator: Kirbi Fagan
Cover Design: Charlee Hoffman
Editor: Matt Sinclair

This is a work of fiction. Names, characters, places, and incidents are either the product of the author's imagination or are used fictitiously, and any resemblance to actual persons living or dead, business establishments, events, or locales is purely coincidental.

Elephant's Bookshelf Press, LLC
Springfield, N.J. 07081
www.elephantsbookshelfpress.com

ISBN-13: 978-1-940180-09-0
Printed in the United States of America.

As a child I often fell asleep to the sound of my dad's IBM Selectric typewriter hammering away on a new manuscript. This book is for him.

At family reunions, my storytellin' relatives would perform live, telling and re-telling hilariously epic family histories, to the delight of everyone. This book is for them.

Now, at home, Barbara and Bella are my joy and motivation. This book is for them.

And finally, this book is for you, whoever you may be. Enjoy it. Share it. Because everyone needs a little magic in their life.

Part One

The Disappearance of Billy Bobble

ONE

The Incident

"You're in a lot of trouble, young lady."

Adults say the stupidest things sometimes. Of course 12-year-old Suzy Quinofski was in trouble. She sat in a police interrogation room covered in dirt and dried tears. Her fingers were cracked and bloody from digging in the ground. She looked like she'd just lost her best friend, because she had. The adult informing her of the obvious was Detective Mark Danner.

Suzy put him straight. "You don't know the half of it." Actually, he didn't know a tenth of it. He didn't know a millionth of it.

"Then why don't you fill me in?"

"Because you couldn't comprehend it if I did."

"Suzy!" Janice Quinofski, a.k.a. Mom, used what

Suzy called her "bad dog!" voice, reserved for those rare occasions when Suzy needed disciplining. Obviously, Mom wasn't accustomed to seeing her sweet, straight-A, multiple-scholarship-contender daughter acting like a street kid. This was a whole new world for both of them.

"What, Mom? It's true." Then to Danner, "No offense. I don't think there's anyone on the planet who could understand it."

"It's not that complicated. I just want to know what happened to Billy."

"I told you. He disappeared."

"Disappeared to where?" asked Danner.

"If I knew that he wouldn't be 'disappeared,' would he?"

"There was an explosion," said Danner.

"No, there was an endoplasmic eruption of what we think might be Bose-Einstein condensate on an OTC scale."

"OTC?"

When Suzy didn't answer, Danner turned to her mother. "Off the chart," she said.

"Out of all of that what you didn't get was OTC?" asked Suzy.

"Maybe I'm not as dumb as you think."

Suzy nodded toward the two-way mirror that filled a wall of the interrogation room. "Maybe you've had too many lawyers complain about abbreviations in your transcripts."

"I told you she was smart."

From behind the mirror, Detective Alan Reins was videotaping the interview. "She's right, by the way."

Dr. Cassandra Weston, a 27-year-old child psychiatrist working off her student loans as a social worker for the state, let out a dismissive but polite, "Yeah."

"A Bose-Einstein what?"

"That's some advanced physics," she said more to herself than Reins.

"Sounds like a stereo system for geeks."

Weston ignored the detective and dug her phone out of her purse. "If I'm going to keep up with her delusions, I'm going to need help."

"Call it what you want," said Danner to Suzy back in the interrogation room. "Something blew up and it took Billy with it."

"Maybe so," said Suzy, "but not in the way you think."

"How then?"

"If Billy exploded his guts would be all over the school yard. Did you find any bloody remains in Linda Lubinski's hair?"

"Suzy! Billy was your friend."

"*Is* my friend, Mom. Billy is my friend, and I wish they would let me out of here so I could help get him back."

"How would you do that?" asked Danner.

She hung her head. "I don't know."

"Okay, good. That was honest. Keep it up and together we can find Billy." Suzy's silence passed as capitulation.

"Your friends have told us—"

"They aren't my friends."

Danner stopped to acknowledge what she said, then went on. "They told us you and Billy were working on some sort of elaborate magic trick."

"Not a trick. Actual magic."

"Hey, I need that honesty. You're smart enough to know there's no such thing as actual magic."

"Okay, if you want to get all Arthur C. Clarke on me: 'Technology advanced to the point of being indistinguishable from magic'—which for you would probably be a cell phone."

"Suzy!"

"That's all right, Mrs. Quinofski. Suzy, you can be as surly and sarcastic as you like, so long as you tell me what happened. How did Billy disappear?"

"It's a long story."

"I get paid by the hour."

"You won't believe me."

"Try me."

"Okay." Suzy glared at him with as cold a stare as she could muster and told the truth. "Billy Bobble made a magic wand."

Two

The Witches of Winston High

SUZY QUINOFSKI TRANSCRIPT
RE: BILLY BOBBLE - MISSING

Billy and I were born to be friends. We even have the same birthday. No one knows Billy better than I do, and that's important because people are going to say he's crazy like his mother, but that's not true. Some will tell you he had a million reasons for blowing up the school, and that's... okay, maybe he did, but what kid doesn't, right? That doesn't mean we do it.

Billy wanted his wishes to come true, like any of us, I guess. The difference is, Billy and I could actually make it happen.

We're both prodigies, which means we're super smart in some things, but completely average in others. That's a dichotomy that can be hard to deal with—like the fact that I'm a 12-year-old who uses words like 'dichotomy.' That'll get you beaten up in the seventh grade, trust me.

But we weren't in the seventh grade. We were the youngest freshmen ever at Winston High. That wasn't a big deal. We'd been the youngest kids in our class since we moved up in first grade, then again in third. Of course, this was high school, and that was a big deal. Everything was different. Some of the kids had their own cars. We had a hard time telling teachers from students, and we didn't exactly blend with the rest of our freshman class.

Not that Billy and I ever blended. They called him "Bobble Head Billy" since kindergarten when he threw a fit because the teacher wouldn't let him demonstrate long division to the class. That was after he'd already shown us addition, subtraction, and the multiplication tables.

Somehow I'd missed out on the nickname Suzy Q. Instead, they called me "Snotski" for no particular reason other than my brains and less than stellar fashion sense. No matter. I hated those kids as much as they hated me.

That's one place Billy and I differ. He likes people, even the bullies. After some jerk tears him a new one, Billy will say, "I feel sorry for that kid. His life must suck to make him so mean." When I tell him to grow a backbone, he says, "I have a backbone, a very flexible one."

"Yeah," I'd say. "Wedgies will do that for you."

Billy got through lower and middle grades by doing the high school kids' math and science homework in exchange for playground protection. Of course, none of the high schoolers were ever around when Billy needed them, but occasionally his generosity with his smarts would pay a dividend. Some punk—or worse, one of the rich kids from Oakridge Prep School—would make the mistake of pounding on Bobble Head in front of the football team. The jocks would come to Billy's rescue, and for a few weeks he would enjoy the safety that gossip can bring.

"Don't mess with Bobble Head, he's a made man."

Of course, none of the kids he helped ever hung out with him, or called him a friend. "No matter," Billy would say, "They'll learn."

"Not if you keep doing their homework for them."

Even before we started high school, Billy and I were King and Queen geeks on campus. Not a bad achievement if you ask me. We hadn't even walked in the front door on our first day when:

"Where do you think you're going, Bobble Head?"

It was Scott Stockwell, senior on the football team, little brother to All-American college quarterback—and academic team, thanks to Billy—Sam. Scott was laughing at his clever turn of phrase.

"Scott, you and every other kid have been calling me that since birth. I think the humor has worn out of it."

That might seem like a lot of bravado for the King of the Geeks, but Billy had long ago learned it was good to be king. He could speak truth to brute.

"Shows what you know. Where's my homework?"

"It's the first day of school, Scott. I don't have your homework."

"What about my summer reading list?"

"You didn't give me your list."

"So?"

"I do math and physics, Scott. You should know that, since I got your brother through college." Billy might seem all touchy-feely and naive to the ways of the world, but he wasn't a complete idiot. He once showed me a list of his worst enemies, the people they feared most, and his relationship to those people. I helped him memorize it so he'd always be able to remind his bullies that he was on good terms with their bullies.

"What am I supposed to do about my reading list?" Scott asked.

Billy walked away from him toward our first class. "I don't know, read them?"

"You are such a freak!"

Billy turned back but kept walking. "Yeah, yeah. We've established in our long, tumultuous relationship that I'm a freak and you're captain of the football team."

"Billy," I whispered. "You need to use your outdoor vocabulary. Remember, polysyllabics are fightin' words to jocks."

Billy turned to walk away, and that's how we bumped into the Witches of Winston High.

Juniors Mary Wane, Linda Lubinski, Lisa Chang, and Sonni More walked down the hall like they owned the place, and as far as Billy was concerned, they did. He'd never admit it, but I'd noticed he was developing a thing for bad girls—and none were badder than the Coven.

Their title as witches was self-proclaimed, as they were openly Wiccan. Billy had a bit of a problem with that. His lifelong dedication to the logic and philosophy of science clashed with his newly formed attention to girls, particularly these girls. Sure, they believed in spells, incantations, and potions and so must be shunned, but:

Mary's golden hair caught the light just right every time. Oh, how I hated that. For boys, she had a smile that revealed a naughty sort of gleam in her eye. For girls, that same smile said, "I'm sorry you're so pathetic."

Linda was gothic, tough, raven-haired, black-lipstick-wearing, pale-skinned trouble—but at least she hated everyone equally. I had to respect her for that.

Lisa Chang never talked out of turn, but her eyes always said, "back off!" which made most boys want to do anything but.

Sonni was playful and fun with a dangerous edge and a mouthful of braces. Her mood could change in a flash.

Billy's intellect didn't stand a chance against the Coven. In fact, he could barely stand—or hold his pile of textbooks. He flat out gawked when they walked by.

Linda noticed and flicked her fingers in his general direction. "Boo!"

That was enough for Billy to lose his balance and his grip, sending to the floor physics and math theory texts that the rest of the class wouldn't see until college—and even then only in the hands of grad students.

But no one was impressed with the quality of what spilled in front of Billy, just the comedy.

"Nice spell," said Sonni.

"You're wicked," said Mary with respect to Linda, who added a saunter to her strut.

A spell had been cast on Billy, all right, but it wasn't anything that hadn't been done to every 12-year-old boy since the dawn of time.

"Does it ever bother you, being a geek?"

Billy had held in his question all day, until our official time to talk. We had walked home together since the third grade. It was something we could count on. No matter how crazy life got, we'd have our little mobile therapy sessions. Sometimes we'd solve the problems of the world. Sometimes we'd complain about teachers, or more often kids. Sometimes we'd help each other with the weighty issues of his crazy single mother, or my stern, but mostly absent father.

"What makes you think I'm a geek?" I said. This was a running joke with us. "Is it my rhinestone cat's-eyes glasses? My dad's old dress shirts and ties, jeans, and army boots?"

"It's your two-hundred and ten IQ."

"Well, you're no better. Look at you. You're skin and bone." It was true. He had no body fat or muscle, lanky limbs and a mop of blonde hair that hadn't seen a comb in a decade.

"Don't forget my IQ."

"Don't go fishing for compliments." I didn't tell him this, but—if he'd learn to stand up straight, he wouldn't be half-bad.

I could tell he was in a mood. "Why do you ask?"

"I don't know." He was quiet for a block. I knew better than to try to drag anything out of him. He'd get there. "It's just that… last year we were the oldest kids in school."

"No we weren't. We were just the head of the class. We're never the oldest."

"Not just that. In grade school helping the high school kids made me, I don't know, kind of cool, you know?"

"In your own dorky way, yes. But nothing's changed about that. The football team will always need your help to get the grades, and they make sure the Oakridge kids pay you instead of beating their homework out of you."

"I guess…"

Oakridge Academy's reputation for powerful alumni can be misleading. Most of their students are rich, not smart. Rich, spoiled, mean, and living in a boarding school. Billy charged them three times what he did public school kids for homework, and the jocks were happy to make sure the preppies paid on time.

"I've been feeling like a chump all day."

"You're a 'Nice Guy,' Billy. Nice Guys are all chumps."

"Oh… thanks."

"Better a chump than a jerk. Trust me."

"Are those my only two choices?"

I thought about it. "Pretty much, yeah."

"It's going to be a long year."

"That could be a good thing, if it's a fun year."

"We'll see."

In fact, it would be a year that would change the world forever. I just hope it's not the last year of Billy Bobble's life.

Three

Billy's Big Wish

"See, her delusions are beginning," said Cassie to the air inside the observation room. "Twelve-year-olds can't change the world."

"If thinking you can change the world makes a 12-year-old crazy," said Detective Reins over the video camera, "then they should lock my daughter up. She thinks she has the world on a string."

"Has she tried to blow it up?"

"Point taken."

SUZY QUINOFSKI TRANSCRIPT - CONTINUED

Billy and I shared study hall and American history with the

Witches of Winston High. Study hall was with Mrs. Nelson, who was deaf as a post, so we'd spend most of the time talking instead of reading. Over time, Billy learned to not stammer or drool while around the coven; I learned not to take it personally, and they learned he'd do pretty much anything they wanted without so much as a nod to the four points of the compass.

Unfortunately, Billy could never quite shut down his intellectual side. Or his mouth.

"You're ascribing a result to a completely unrelated action." He'd barged into a conversation they were having about a spell concocted to postpone an English test.

"'Ascribe?' I've never 'ascribed' anything in my life," said Sonni.

"Billy, you are such a dork," said Linda. "Just shut up and finish my math homework."

Billy reached into his briefcase and pulled out two printed pages of algebra and handed it to Linda. "For every action there is an equal and opposite reaction," he said.

"Exactly," said Linda instead of thank you. "Our spell created the desired reaction."

"No, that would be for *any* action there is some other action that you decide is a *re*action."

The Coven all stared at him like he'd farted. Finally, Lisa Chang spoke. "Shut up, Billy."

"I'm just saying…"

"Shut up, Billy," said the four girls together.

"…It's physics."

"Shut up, Billy," said the entire study hall. Except me.

✳

"Why do you even talk to those girls?"

I got a smirk from the soldier on duty at the Army base's gate. Having a top general for a father meant I lived in two completely different worlds. On base and off. Off, I was like every other kid. On, I was part of the royal family. We got the best housing the government had to offer—even if Dad was rarely home to enjoy it—and I got forty-three thousand loyal soldiers looking out for me. Not always a plus.

Billy had been enough a part of my on-base life to seamlessly move from one world to the other. Talking about girls made him blush a little as he passed the guard, but he stayed on topic. "I don't know."

"I do." He talked to the coven for the same reason I wanted to talk to Johnny Jet. The same reason every girl wanted to talk to Jet. When I think about it, I had to give Billy props for his courage, but still—"They treat you like dirt, Billy."

"I know, but…"

"Better to be treated like dirt than have them not know you're alive?"

"I don't want to talk about it."

"Look, Billy." I stopped. Was I really about to give him advice on women? "If you want to talk to a girl, it's not a good idea to bad mouth her religion."

"But…"

"But nothing. They're Wiccan. It might be crap to you and me but it's an established, recognized religion."

"But it doesn't make sense."

"So? If you wanted to go out with Christian Chrissy Swenson would you tell her that talking snakes and reducing the gene pool for the entire animal kingdom down to two mating pairs per species was ridiculous?"

Billy pouted for a second, then: "Well… it is."

"You're impossible."

"And yet, I exist nonetheless."

I shot him a crooked smile. "I'll be glad when you get better taste in women."

"Shut up. I'm twelve."

"What? Girls still have cooties?"

"Shut up, I said."

We got to my house, where Billy usually came in to hang out, but this time he stopped at the sidewalk. "You coming in?"

"No, you're coming over to my place."

"I am?"

"The new RAM for your laptop is waiting at my doorstep."

Billy lived with his mother and brother in the trailerhood—mobile homes outside the Army base. He joked that it's "Trailer Trash Chic," when in fact the house and yard were a visible representation of his mother's twisted mental state.

From what his mom told me, she married right out of high school to a buck private she thought might become an officer. Depending on which story she was in the mood to tell, she either threw him out, or he left her high and dry. Either way, the fact was he wasn't around, but Billy and his big brother, Peter, were. Whether she was crazy before he left or got that way afterward, I don't know—but trust me, she's not all there.

Apparently she never talked to Billy about his father. Billy and I did. Once. He said his grandmother told him the story before she died, and that's all he ever said about it. Ever. We had a don't-ask/don't-tell policy on the subject, as it was obvious by his silence that it bothered him. It bothered me that my dad was always halfway around the world in dangerous situations, but at least I could send him an e-mail or talk to him online; hear him say that he loved me.

Billy wasn't so lucky. The issue was our constant invisible companion, the elephant in the room no one ever talked about, and it was sitting on Billy's chest.

When we got to the door of his trailer, there was no package waiting.

"Peter!" he shouted.

I could hear Peter in his makeshift shop in the side yard working on the love of his life, a '67 Dodge Charger that he'd tricked out beyond belief. At 19-years-old, he could move out anytime he wanted, but his job as a junior mechanic didn't pay him enough to be totally on his own. He'd never admit it, but I think he had other reasons to stay.

"I'm busy!" he shouted back.

Generally speaking, Peter was as cool as Billy was not—a fact that made them jealous of each other. Being boys they never discussed it. They used to fight and snap all the time. Finally, they stopped talking as much as two people can who share a house with an unstable woman.

"I was expecting a package," said Billy.

"Yeah. I signed for it and put it in your room."

"You're not allowed in my room!"

"I slid it under your door."

This entire conversation was shouted from front yard to back, but it was still more than I heard them say to each other in years.

So the package was inside. Billy didn't want to go inside. Not with me there. He stood in front of the door and stared at the knob.

"You could give me your computer," he said to the door. "I can bring it back to you tonight."

"Don't be silly, Billy, you don't want to walk all the way back."

He didn't say anything. He didn't move, just kept staring at the knob.

"It's okay, Billy, I've been in your house before."

"Every time I open this door," he said, "I make a wish. Do you know what I wish for?"

"That it'll be clean inside?"

"That was my big wish. The granddaddy of them all, but I've given up on that. I just wish I could open it wide enough to walk in like a real person."

"Well, Billy, some real people are hoarding junk collectors like your Mom, so in that sense, your wish is granted."

He finally looked at me with the saddest puppy dog eyes. "You want to wait out here?"

I could have, but I didn't want him to think I was afraid of how he lived—or, rather, how his mother lived. "No, I'm fine. I helped clean it out before."

"That was three years ago."

"So?"

"Fine," said Billy. He opened the door. It moved about three inches then jammed on something behind it. He slammed his shoulder against it and pushed.

"Careful of my stuff," came the slurry voice of his mother from inside the dark abyss.

"Your stuff is junk, Mom!" Billy wedged the door open another foot and said, "That'll have to do."

"It's fine." I squeezed inside after him.

Obviously, besides being a depressed alcoholic, Billy's mom was a hoarder, which is why we didn't spend a lot of time at his house. Billy and Peter had managed to cut paths through the mess to get from one room to another, but that was about it. The rest was uselessness piled to the ceilings.

"Oh, you've got your friend with you," Mrs. Bobble said when she saw me. She sat in her little corner watching a talk show on a six-inch TV. She still had on her Wal-Mart vest from work, and a once-white-now-yellowish slip. "Sorry for the mess. I've been meaning to straighten up, but… you know how it is."

"Oh, it's fine." I lied. It wasn't fine, but that was all I could say without gagging.

"Would you like to stay for dinner? We could dig out another place for you."

"No, uh—"

"Mom, she doesn't want to stay for dinner. No one wants to stay in this garbage pit any longer than they have to."

Go, Billy! Normally, he was the sweetest kid you'd ever want to meet, but when it came to his family, he would lash out with cruel honesty. Not that I blamed him. "Hold your breath," he told me. "There's fresh air in my room."

I followed him over a mound of laundry, around a pile of decaying newspapers, and waited while he opened the padlock on his door.

"It's the only way I can keep her clutter out," he said.

Both boys kept their space immaculately clean. Billy's was downright sparse, with nothing but a single bed, a desk, and a chair. That's it. He had his clothes in the closet, his computer dock on the desk, but nothing else.

"I keep all my stuff in my head," he always said.

It didn't take long to install the RAM into my laptop. I needed it to boost the graphics for a DNA simulation I was working on. Billy rebooted it and ran more than enough tests to make sure it was working. I could tell he didn't want to leave the sanctity of his room, but eventually we had to, and sure enough ran into Billy's mom on our way out. She'd moved to the deck, where she liked to sit and drink.

"You be careful going home," she said. "They're watching you."

"She thinks the gnomes are spies," Billy told me with a point to the neighbor's yard. Sure enough, their yard gnomes faced our way.

"They tell the others what's going on. Not that they need them. They know all about what's happening. And they'll gitcha when the sun goes down."

"That's right, Mom," said Billy, "which is why Suzy had best be on her way."

"Don't be caught out at night!"

Billy said to me, "Don't listen to her. Just go."

"Will you be okay?" I asked. I don't know why. What would I do if he said no?

"Why should tonight be different from any other? She'll pass out soon enough."

"Okay, well… thanks for the help." I didn't know what else to say. What do you say in a situation like that?

"It's no wonder the kid blew up his school," said Dr. Weston. She drew a line down the middle of her notepad and labeled the columns "Billy" and "Suzy." She had two patients now. One alive, on the other side of the glass in front of her, and one missing, presumed dead.

Four

A Bully by Any Other Gnome

SUZY QUINOFSKI TRANSCRIPT - CONTINUED

"Forty bucks," said Billy to Brad Hopkins. He was an Oakridge Boy, a preppy senior who wanted to graduate in the spring to avoid summer school for the first time in his life. We were in the courtyard at lunch.

"But you do Stockwell's homework for free."

"Stockwell can and will beat the crap out of me. I don't think you have it in you."

"Try me."

"Stockwell and his friends will happily beat the crap out of any of you Oakridge kids who lay a hand on me, Hopkins, so either pay up, or go home. You're trespassing."

"You suck, Bobble Head."

"Dr. Seaver's chem. 101 homework for a week for forty bucks. I think that's a pretty good deal."

Hopkins handed over the money, and Billy gave him five pages of chemistry equations. "Don't share them with anyone else, or I'll cut the whole school off cold. And make sure you don't turn it all in at once, will you?"

"I know the deal." Everyone knew the deal when it came to buying homework from Billy. Hopkins inspected the equations as if to see if they were quality work.

Billy turned them right side up for him. "Good luck with that."

"You suck, Bobble Head."

"I'll take that as a 'thank you.'"

When Billy sat back down at the geek's table, Doug Crone said, "I don't know why you spend all of your time doing their homework."

"I don't. I haven't since the third grade. The teachers all give the same assignments, so I reprint from the previous year. Easy money."

"You're completely ruining social Darwinism, you know?" I had made that joke with Billy before, but the rest of our crowd hadn't heard it. "You should let their kind die out as nature intended."

The laughs from my audience were cut short when Scott Stockwell shouted something rude at the Coven from across the yard.

"Speaking of devolution," I said under my breath.

"I'm sorry," said Scott. We all recognized the tone. Scott was angry, maybe even drunk. "I meant to say, 'witches.'"

The Coven, who were apparently practicing a spell in

the far corner of the courtyard—holding hands in a circle and mumbling—didn't respond except to chant louder.

"Why don't they just wear a sign that says, 'Make Fun of Us'?" I asked Billy.

But he was more curious about Scott's condition. "What's gotten into him?"

"You didn't hear?" Obviously not. "He was cut from the football team."

"Really?"

"Steroids."

"Is he crazy?"

"Apparently."

"Doesn't he know that'll kill him?"

"Apparently not."

Scott was still focused on the four girls. "Whacha doin'? Praying?"

"He should have had the girls say a spell for *him*," I told Billy. "Would have been just as effective as the steroids without the liver cancer."

"You trying to cast a spell? ... to turn me into a pig, or something?"

We geeks shared the same look, *Too late for that*, though none of us was dumb enough to say it out loud.

"You prayin' to your witch-god? You prayin' to Satan? You *are* prayin' to Satan! That's just wrong."

"They aren't praying, you idiot."

Billy was on his feet. Scott turned his bile toward him like a tank's turret, and the focus of every kid in the courtyard turned with him. Billy's lesser friends backed away quickly.

I tried to stay by his side, but my feet crept backwards.

"What are you doing?"

"'What have I done?' would be a better way of putting it."

Scott steamed toward Billy until they were nose-to-chest. "What did you say?"

"I assume that you're not interested in a discussion about the complete lack of disparity between prayer and spells." Billy waved words before Stockwell like a red cape in front of a charging bull.

It worked. "What!?"

"You said they are praying to Satan. That's not a conclusion you can draw from four girls sitting in a circle, or maybe along the points of the compass, and chanting. I mean, who knows, it might be a Buddhist thing."

"You are such a *freak*!"

"Yes, we've established that over our long and sordid history. I am a freak and you are…" I saw the briefest flash of emotion in Scott's eyes—first sadness, then a mortal fear. Billy must have seen it too, because he pressed on. "You are what?"

Scott was no longer captain of the football team. Their long history had changed. Billy had the upper hand. In all the time I'd known them, Billy had never been in this position before. He could reduce his mortal enemy to tears right there in front of the entire school. He could have done to Stockwell emotionally what had been done to him physically by so many bullies so many times in his life. Should he have done it? I would have.

But that's another place where Billy and I differ. He let him off the hook. "You are Scott."

Stockwell wasn't sure what just happened, but Billy's

tone suggested he might have been given a way out of this potential humiliation. "That's right!" he said, but his bravado rang false. "And don't you forget it." He stormed off and I could see the sun flash off the moisture in his eyes.

The hush that fell over the entire courtyard lunch break slowly eroded with the chatter of did-you-see-that's and I-can't-believe-it's, me among them. "Nice conflict avoidance."

"Our spell saved you." Linda Lubinski and the rest of the Coven had made their way across the courtyard and circled Billy like he was a May Pole.

"You're lucky," said Mary.

"If it wasn't for us," said Sonni.

"You'd be dead." Lisa completed the sentence.

Billy's tongue was just shy of hanging out of his mouth like a dog's, so Linda gave him some advice. "Say 'thank you.'"

"Thank you."

"All too easy," said Linda as she led the girls away.

I watched them go. "Scott was right. They are ... that word that rhymes with 'witches.'"

"Are you insane?"

Billy had pitched part of his new thoughts to me that day on our walk home.

"No, I think it's possible."

"Those are two diametrically opposed positions, Billy. You can't be sane and think that's possible."

"Why not? Why aren't you getting this? It's so simple.

What is magic?"

"You mean besides Clarke's definition of advanced technology?"

"That definition doesn't entirely work. If it's technology advanced enough to be indistinguishable from magic, what is the technology doing to make it appear to be magic?"

"I don't know."

Billy took me by the arm with more fortitude than I thought him capable of. "Exactly. So, we need to define what it's doing. We need to define magic."

"Okay." I wondered if he'd gotten taller.

"Let's say that magic is…" He let go of my arm and started walking in the wrong direction. "…seemingly unrelated cause and effect."

"'Seemingly?' Are you trying to tell me—"

Billy interrupted to clarify. "You say a spell and suddenly an anvil falls on your enemy's head."

"Or Scott Stockwell leaves you alone."

"What? Oh. Yeah, nothing to do with that, but whatever."

Yeah, right.

"Unrelated cause and effect. Something happens by magic. Something happens by seemingly unrelated cause and effect."

"Are you saying that they aren't unrelated?"

"Oh, in that case, of course not. The spell has nothing to do with the anvil."

"Or Stockwell."

"Uh, yeah… whatever. All I'm saying is that it is scientifically possible to create seemingly unrelated cause and effect to the point that it would appear to be—or, by definition *actually be*—magic. Real magic."

"Well that answers my first question." I left him standing there like the dork that he was.

"What?"

"You are definitely insane."

My second question—about whether or not he'd gotten taller—remained unanswered.

After hanging out at my house eating chocolate Pop Tarts with peanut butter until the fall sun went down, Billy said he had to go home. I decided to walk with him. I don't remember what we talked about along the way. Nothing important, I'm sure. I do remember Billy's anxiety when he saw them.

The red and blue police lights bouncing off the aluminum siding of his trailerhood was not an uncommon sight, but we both slowed our pace. His brother had stayed out of trouble for years. We shared an unspoken fear that he might have slipped back into bad habits, but that wasn't the case. Not this time.

"Don't let them take my baby!"

It was his mother. With the dread of responsibility that birth into the wrong family can bring, Billy ran toward the lights. I was right behind him.

His mother's ongoing battle with the neighbor's yard gnomes had come to blows. She always promised to get revenge on the little clay men for… whatever it was they were supposed to have done.

"She'll never do it for real," Peter once told me.

"That's why she always waits until we're nearby before trying it."

Apparently, she hadn't waited this time. Billy found her in her ratty old nightgown standing in the rubble of broken figurines, with another one in her hand ready to smash to the ground, while two uniformed officers surrounded her, with taser and mace ready.

"Put the yard gnome down," shouted the lady cop.

"They want to take my baby!"

"Mom!" Billy ran toward the scene. "I'm right here, Mom. I'm fine."

"Run, baby! Run away. They want you, Billy." Just as the officer turned to see Billy sprinting toward her, Billy's mother charged the lady officer's back, with the heavy decoration raised to attack.

"Mom, stop!" Billy flew past the cop to grab the gnome. As he did, the other officer fired his taser at the crazy lady assaulting his partner, but Mrs. Bobble tripped over broken pieces of gnomes. When she fell, the taser darts hit Billy square in the chest.

I imagine that somewhere in his head equations of Amps, Joules and volts ran rampant trying to avoid the inevitable. Then every muscle in his body contracted simultaneously, and he crashed to the ground. To make matters worse, Mrs. Bobble got up with the gnome-weapon, more determined than ever to use it. The female cop had no choice but to let loose with her pepper spray which rained down on Billy's face as well. The instant the taser let go its electric grip on Billy's body, he vomited chocolate pop tarts and peanut butter all down his shirt.

The male cop struggled to cuff Mrs. Bobble, who

straddled her son. Her eyes were puffing up full and red. Tears streamed from them as did junk from her nose and mouth. "Don't listen to them, baby," she screamed. "Don't do what they say."

Then she vomited all over her baby's face.

Billy's muscles were still twitching, so there was nothing he could do. Mercifully, the cops lifted him out of the puddle of sick to his feet.

"You all right?" one of them asked.

Before he could answer a girl's voice behind me said, "That's a new look for you, Billy." It was Linda Lubinski from the coven.

"Oh, God," said Billy. His legs went limp for a second, surely from the humiliation.

The cops took his weight and misinterpreted his stumbling. "We should take him to the hospital," said the guy.

"Her too," said the woman. "Psych for sure." They walked Billy right past Linda on the way to their squad car.

I expected her to laugh at him. I knew he could take that. He'd been laughed at plenty of times in his life. What I didn't expect was pity. That was quickly replaced with the unmistakable "OMG that's disgusting" crinkle of her face, and a hand to her nose as the smell of pepper spray, vomit, and other foul bodily fluids that Billy no doubt had lost to the tasing.

"Drive!" I heard him say to the officers when they rolled down the back windows. "Please, just go!"

But even that relief didn't come quickly, as the cops had to collect his mother and get contact information from witnesses—including me and Linda.

"Where are you taking him?" I asked.

"The emergency room. He's fine, it's just a precaution."

"Call Peter," said Billy from the back of the car. I told the officers that Peter was his 19-year-old brother and that we would meet them at the hospital.

Finally, the cops got in the car and were about to drive away, when Billy said, "Linda?"

She turned.

"Say a spell for me?"

She scoffed. "You don't believe in them."

"Please?" He meant it. I could tell. If believing in little old ladies on flying broomsticks and unicorns could somehow create an alternate universe where his mother wasn't a drunk and he wasn't covered in vomit in the backseat of a police car, then so be it.

Linda must have sensed his desperation, and even she wasn't mean enough to kick a kid who was this down. "Sure," she said. "One get out of jail free spell coming up."

Five

Make the Connection

SUZY QUINOFSKI TRANSCRIPT - CONTINUED

Of the two Bobble brothers, Peter was the one who knew the world of criminal justice. He explained to me on the ride to the hospital that Billy wasn't the one in trouble. "Cops accidentally tased a 12-year-old honor student," he said. "They're going to be hearing from my attorney." Of course, Peter's attorney had always been a public defender, so it was an empty threat.

We found Billy waiting in the emergency room. He looked so sad sitting in a corner by himself covered in yuck and pepper spray. Part of me wanted to give him a hug and say everything would be all right, and part of me wanted to stand as far away as possible with a fire hose and body wash. The other people-in-waiting must have agreed with the latter, because though the room was full, every seat in a ten foot radius around Billy was empty.

To his credit, Peter didn't let Billy's condition phase him a bit. He plopped down in the seat next to his little brother, put his feet up on a table and said, "How are the magazine's in this place?" When Billy didn't say anything, Peter picked one up and checked the cover. "Chevy introduces the Volt," he read. "Old. Why are they always so old?"

"Are you sure you want to sit next to me?" Billy asked. His voice was barely audible.

"Of course I don't want to sit next to you. You're a complete dork and I'm ashamed to be seen with you."

"Yeah, and I reek of vomit and pepper spray."

"Hey, for the kids I used to hang with, that's like perfume." He gave me a nod and somehow I knew what he wanted. I tossed him a trash bag that held a fresh change of clothes for Billy. Peter had been very specific about packing them in the plastic. "There's clothes in here for you," he told Billy. "First, get undressed. Then wash your hands, your face and any skin that might have pepper spray on it. Use a lot of soap, okay?"

"Okay."

"Only when you think you're clean do you open the bag and get dressed. Put your dirty clothes in the bag. Don't let the smelly stuff touch the clean stuff. Tie it back tight, okay?"

"Okay."

Peter gave him the sack, but Billy didn't move. Peter flipped through another magazine like he didn't care, but I saw him glancing sideways to check in on him. Finally

Billy asked, "How did you get into my room to get my clothes?"

"Magic," he said. "Bathroom's over there. You're not bleeding, so you have plenty of time before they call you in."

He wasn't wrong about that. We waited for hours. Billy left the bag of old clothes in the trash in the bathroom. "Bad smells, bad memories," he said.

He'd have more of both before the night was over.

Once he got the okay from the ER doctor, we went up to see his mother. She was being held in the psych ward pending a hearing to determine if she might be a harm to herself or others. I felt like I was walking into a movie. An orderly escorted us into an elevator, swiped a card across a security scanner, pressed the button for the third floor and told us to turn left once we got off, but that wasn't entirely necessary. The arresting officers were waiting for us.

They lead us through the security doors that closed off the ward from the rest of the building, and explained that, technically, Billy's mom should have been taken to the police station, but considering the tasing they thought they'd bring her here.

"Trust us, a couple of nights here beats jail," said the male officer. "We bring in crazies all the time, and they don't do well without meds in the general population. It's not good."

"Not that we're saying your mother is crazy," said the woman.

"Please," said Peter. "She's been ready for the short bus for a long time."

"Mr. Bobble," said one of the doctors.

"I think he means you," I told Peter, since neither of the young misters took notice.

"Yes?"

The doctor waved him over for a private conversation.

Billy and I sat quietly in the lobby. Patients roamed around mumbling to themselves and occasionally staring at us. I had to wonder, what was it about these mentally ill people that gave me a creepy feeling inside. All the journals I studied said they weren't any different from someone with cancer or a broken leg or something, but I wouldn't feel uncomfortable around those people. Why did I feel that way with psych patients? This could become a problem for me, since my favorite subject was microbiology as it relates to brain diseases.

Billy rocked in his seat. "I wish. I wish. I wish."

"What are you mumbling?"

"I think I know now why people believe in magic. I wish I could make this day go away."

"I wish I was a *real* boy," I teased. Sure, Billy had problems, some of them pretty big, but I came from a military family. We weren't allowed to feel sorry for ourselves, and I wasn't going to let Billy do it either. "Look, Pinocchio," I said, "you see that water fountain over there?"

"Yeah."

"You push the button on that water fountain, and—for free—you'll get fresh, clean, water. They've even chilled it for you to just the right temperature."

"What's your point?"

"Most people on the planet don't have fresh water. They have to walk for miles, or dig a well, and carry it back to their homes. It takes half a day to get what you get by pushing a little button, so what do you have to feel sorry about? Really?"

Billy sat in silence for a moment, then said, "Your dad gave you that speech didn't he?"

Okay, I was busted. "About a thousand times."

"Did you hate it as much coming from him as I did coming from you?"

"Yeah, probably. Doesn't make it any less true, though."

Billy looked past the wandering patients at the water fountain. "I wish I could push a button and make my mom not crazy."

"Wishing can make it so." One of the patients sat down next to Billy and started speaking a mile a minute. "Make a wish. What is a wish? A wish is a thought. Thoughts. What are thoughts? Bio-chemical electrical impulses in the brain. And electricity is a thing. It's real. It's tangible. You can touch it. BBBZZZZZZZ! Don't touch it; it hurts. But if A equals B and so on, then there you have it. Wishes are real. Make a wish. It's real."

"That's not what the boy needs to hear," said another patient who was as really old and just as intense as the other guy, without being excitable. "There is a connection. The connection is reality. You have to break it to make your wishes come true." Funny, but if this old man hadn't been in a patient's gown and black socks, I'd have said he didn't belong. He seemed more like a great grandfather than a mental case.

"Yes, yes, yes," said the excitable one. "There is a connection to all things. You are connected to your family. You're connected to your job. That can be a good thing or a bad thing, you feel me? You feel what I'm saying to you?"

This was getting creepy. The patients who had been floating around minding their own business started to take an interest in us.

The older patient ignored the others, speaking to Billy as if passing on sage advice. "You have to break that connection so you can reconnect reality the way you want it. I am connected to this hospital. You have to break the connection to set yourself free."

"Yes, yes, yes," said the hyper one again. "That's what they want. That's what they need, boy."

"We need you to break the connection," said the old one. "We need you to set us free."

"Set us free," said a couple of the gathering patients.

"That's what they want, boy," the old guy seemed to be leading the show now. "That's what they need. They need you to break the connection. Give them access."

"Break the connection and all things are possible," said hyper boy. "Break the connection and all things are possible."

While the rest of the ward pressed in on us like bad zombies, the old guy turned to me and with complete, sane clarity whispered, "He's going to need your help."

Six

Break the Connection

Dr. Anton Menaus, the 47-year-old professor of quantum physics at Oakridge Academy who Dr. Weston had called, arrived shortly after his cologne.

"Dr. Menaus, thanks for coming."

"You're not a student anymore, Cassie, you can call me Anton."

I'd rather not, thought Weston, as Menaus had a reputation that fit his hipper-than-thou persona. Being around him always left her with a strong desire to take a shower. Still, he was the only quantum physics expert in this military town, so she had no choice but to deal with him.

"I heard about the explosion on the news, but they didn't give any details."

"You ever hear of a kid named 'Billy Bobble'?" she asked.

"Sure. I know Billy. He's been using my lab at Oakridge since he was six."

"Well, he was the cause of the explosion."

"Really?"

"And he's gone missing."

Detective Reins spoke up from behind his video camera. "We're going to want to talk to you about what he was doing in your lab."

"Sure, sure, no problem. I mean, mostly he was borrowing textbooks, working on equations, and doing experiments, something with extreme cold. Lately, he'd spent a lot of time in the biology lab with a friend of his."

"Her?" asked Reins, indicating Suzy through the mirror.

Anton took notice of his surroundings for the first time. "Yes, she's familiar."

"She's the one I need help with," said Weston.

"Sure, sure, no problem."

SUZY QUINOFSKI TRANSCRIPT - CONTINUED

The hospital thing was completely creepy. Orderlies had to escort us out of the lobby and behind the locked gate. I can still hear Billy's mom as we passed her room. "Don't do what they say, Baby. Don't let them take my baby."

Peter told us on the drive home that she had enough sedatives to put a race horse to sleep for a week, but the commotion got her up and agitated again. That's when the doctor and the cops agreed it was best to leave her until morning. She was Peter's problem now. His entrée into adulthood.

It was nearly two in the morning before I lay my head on my pillow, but there would be no doubt we'd be in school the next day. Being geek royalty does come with its responsibilities.

You'd have to be his best friend to notice how the night's adventures had changed Billy. He tried to laugh it off when the story made it around school. "You haven't lived until you've been tased *and* pepper sprayed," he'd say, but the faux smile faded faster than usual, and his eyes carried more than a lack of sleep.

The last thing he needed to hear was Principal Dillon's voice over the school's intercom. "Billy Bobble, could you come to the office, please?"

"You're getting to be a real troublemaker, Billy," said Linda.

"Why did it have to be during study hall?" Billy whispered to me as he gathered his books.

"Want us to conjure another spell for you?" asked Sonni.

We were getting used to the Coven speaking in groups of four, so we waited out Mary and Lisa's requests for a thank you.

"I will say," said Billy, "thank you for thinking of me—which is what a spell or a prayer, or whatever, is—a moment to think about someone else, hopefully in a good way."

"And thoughts are real. Electricity," I said. Our new inside joke.

Linda ignored me, as usual. "Come on, Billy."

"Our spell worked," said Sonni.

"There's no denying it." That was Mary.

"You wouldn't be here if it didn't," said Lisa.

"Do you girls ever talk out of turn?" I said. "Billy never went to jail because—"

"Of our spell." So Linda was listening.

"Billy Bobble, please—" The bell rang, drowning out all conversation and the rest of Principal Dillon's request.

"I'll walk with you to the office," I said. "I have to go clear up some stuff about the marching band." That was true, but I really wanted to keep my eye on him. He was wound tighter than the sweat pants on a Biggest Loser contestant.

"Hey, Billy, the principal is looking for you." A thousand kids must have said that as we made our way toward the office. Their glee at the thought of Billy in trouble gushed like pus from their zits.

"Principal Dillon," announced Billy the minute he opened the door to the office. "The next time you need me, could you send a note? Or call me, like you used to."

The ever-present row of kids waiting to get yelled at by the vice principal tensed, expecting that this little freshman was about to get his head handed to him for speaking to Dillon like that.

Instead, Dillon put down the intercom microphone he was about to use and said, "I'm sorry, Billy, but it's an emergency."

The kids in trouble shifted in their seats. Not the reaction they expected.

"Is it my Mom?" asked Billy.

"No. No. It's the program. It's acting up again."

Billy exasperated. "What did you do?"

"Nothing," said Dillon, making it hard to tell who was the student, and who the teacher. "I didn't touch it. I never touch it, not after last time."

"Mrs. Dillon?" Billy asked the principal's secretary and wife.

"He touched it," she said.

"Well, I wanted to see how it worked. This is my school, after all, and I have a right to know how things work around here."

"Show me what you did." Billy walked over to Mrs. Dillon's desk, which she vacated immediately.

"I just…" said Mr. Dillon, "I just… I didn't do anything. I just… I had this compulsion. I don't know what came over me. I just really, really, wanted to know how the whole thing worked, so I deleted one of these little lines, I think, and it went crazy."

"Which little line?"

"I… I… I don't know, that's the problem."

"You disconnected a link, Mr. Dillon. That's bad. That's very bad."

"Yes, but, if you could explain *why* it's bad, I'd have a better understanding."

"You never had to understand it before."

"I know. I know. But for some reason I'm feeling very insecure about not knowing, so if you could just explain it to me."

"Okay," said Billy, "I'll give it a try." I noticed his jaw tighten and his hands flex. On a good day Billy had a low tolerance for ignorance, and this was far from a good day. "The system is a relational database, right?"

"Right," said Mr. Dillon.

"Do you know what that means?"

"Not a clue."

"Okay. Think of the data in different worlds, with different creatures living in them. In one world, labeled 'Students,' you've got names. Only students' names can live in that world, okay?" He was pushing it, talking to Dillon almost like the principal was a child.

"Another world is labeled 'Guardians,' with addresses, contact information—this is where the parents live, right?"

"Right, I get that."

"In another world, we have 'Classes,' with times, locations, etc. None of this makes sense unless it's connected. Each student is connected to their guardian, their classes, their teachers, their grades, etc. The Fry twins have one address, one set of parents. If the parents move, then you only have to change the data once. And it works because it's all connected. Parent to student to class to teacher to grade. All connected with these little lines, which you deleted. You broke the connection."

"I know, I'm sorry."

"You've created a Cartesian Product."

"I have? What's that?"

"It's when each piece of data in one world is connected to *every* piece of data in the other worlds. Look at this." Billy typed up a quick query. "Here I am, the son of every parent in the city, taking remedial algebra. In what universe do I take remedial anything?"

"I don't know."

"In what universe do I live in such a ritzy neighborhood?"

"I don't know, just please-"

"And the grades. I'm listed five times, with a different grade for each listing. There I am with an F. Is that possible? By what dark magic can I get an F in remedial algebra?"

"I get it," said Mr. Dillon. "I messed up. Could you please just fix it?"

But Billy wasn't listening. "By what magic?" I knew that look. He was thinking.

"I don't know what magic. I broke the connection. I'm sorry," said Mr. Dillon. "Just do do that computer voodoo that you do so well."

"Break the connection and all things are possible," Billy said to the air around him.

"What?"

"The connection is reality. Fixed in reality. Break the connection so you can reconnect to alternate realities. Break the connection and all things are possible."

"No, reconnect it. We don't want all things to be possible, we want the *right* things to be possible, please. Make it normal again. Put the school back together."

"What if I don't want to make it normal?"

"Billy, please, don't talk like that. You know we can't afford a real programmer."

"What if I want to mix things up a little bit?"

"Billy!"

"Make a little unrelated cause and effect."

"Billy!" That was me. I knew the pressure he'd been through the past few days. He hadn't talked about it. He hadn't shown any sign of emotion. Surely, he was about to snap.

He stared at me hard like, *how dare you interrupt my nervous breakdown?* I'd never seen him like this. Come to think of it, I'd never seen him show much of any kind of emotion at all except when they changed companions on *Dr. Who*. He turned from me back to the computer screen and glared at it. Then he grabbed the mouse and clicked the close X on the database. "Save changes?" he asked Mr. Dillon when the prompt came up.

"Um... yes?"

Billy shook his head and clicked "No."

"I've figured it out!"

Billy had been on a low simmer of thought until our walk home. I was glad he finally spoke up, but I played it coy. "I'm supposed to know what you're talking about?"

"How to create magic."

"That taser short-circuited your brain." I decided that making light of the past events was better than pretending they didn't happen.

"What? No. Doesn't matter. It was those crazy people."

"You."

"Very funny. No. Well, maybe, who knows? Anyway, what they said, that we're all connected. That the connection is the thing."

"What about it?"

"You know about Multi-World Theory, right?"

"That billions of universes are created and destroyed

every time anyone anywhere makes a decision about anything?"

"Yeah."

"In other words, crap."

"Well, maybe. Maybe it just needs a little tweaking."

"Like how?" My interest in quantum physics was mild compared to microbiology, but who was I to dam up my friend's stream of consciousness?

"Like what if there's only one universe that's packed with all of those endless possibilities?"

"You're losing me."

"Let me go back." He stopped walking and I wondered if he was literally going to go down the street to pick up an idea he'd dropped. He didn't. "Multi-World Theory says that when I stopped walking, another universe came into existence where I didn't stop. In that universe, maybe I walk right into traffic, get hit by a car and die, while in this universe I live happily ever after."

"But you're saying…?"

He started walking again. "I'm saying that there is only one me, one you, one of everything that takes up space, but there are infinite units of time that each of these objects might be connected to."

"Again, lost."

"We live in linear time, right? One moment follows the next and the next and the next, and they are all lined up in a rigid order."

"Yeah, so?"

"So, physical space is somehow linked to linear time, like the school's database. What if we could break the link?"

"What link?"

"The link, the little line in the database, only instead of being between students and classes, this one is between Space and Time."

"You want to disconnect Space from Time?"

"Yes. To create a Cartesian Product between two infinite sets."

"I have no idea what you just said."

"Every possible Space related to every possible Time—even times from alternate realities. Cause separated from effect. Magic."

We'd gotten to my house, so I tried to get Billy to get to the point. "You haven't answered my question. What is the link?"

That stopped him. "I didn't say I had it *all* figured out."

I felt bad about that, so I tried to get him started again. "So we, all of us –"

"Everything ... or maybe every living thing. I'm not sure about inanimate objects. How does a rock interpret Time?" Billy teetered on the abyss of a tangent.

I kept him grounded. "Right, okay. Everything has something about it that connects it to, like, a database of Time?"

"Right."

"What would this something look like?"

"If it's like a database..." Billy drifted for a second, then, "a database has ID numbers unique to each set. They're called key numbers. When you put them together one part of the number is the same for everything—that's the main set—the other part is unique to the thing itself, that's the subset. So this key would be in two parts. The

Time part would be the same for everything, and the individual part would be completely unique."

"So to work magic…?"

"There are infinite alternate Time choices out there. So we could find the Time where things are the way we want them, and change the Time part of the key. We could find somewhere unicorns and dragons actually evolved. Somewhere broomsticks can be made of a substance immune to gravity. Somewhere… somewhere my mother isn't crazy and my father didn't run away."

He got quiet after that. I didn't say anything for a while, until: "Wanna come in?"

"I want to make magic."

Of course he did. "Might as well. We don't have anything else to do this afternoon."

"Real magic."

"Is there any other kind?"

Billy had dinner with us that night, which was nothing out of the ordinary. When Mom asked, "What have you kids been up to?" Billy leapt into his new theory of actual magic with an explanation of counter-spinning quarks.

"Quarks are teeny, tiny, infinitesimally small particles that come in pairs. They come into existence in pairs and they cannot be destroyed no matter what, until they slam into each other again. And they spin. They spin in one direction or the other, but here's the thing; if you change the direction of one of the particles, the other one changes its direction instantaneously. And I mean that literally. No matter how far apart you separate those two particles, you change the spin on one, the other follows suit."

I know that sounds boring, but you have to picture Billy telling it to you. He gets all excited and talks really fast, like he's describing some kind of race, or boxing match or something. Half the time even I don't know what he's talking about, but he's so energetic and into it that it's fun just to listen.

"Now, here's another thing. We human beings can't travel the speed of light."

"No. Nothing can travel the speed of light." Sometimes I had to remind him that I wasn't as ignorant about Einsteinian physics as he might think. "And we know what quarks are."

"I don't."

"Thanks, Mom. You don't have to encourage him."

"They sound kind of romantic." She smiled at me and Billy when she said, "Two particles that come into the world together and can't be destroyed by anything except each other."

"Mom!"

"You guys are missing the point," Billy said, but he was the one missing Mom's point. Not that that was a revelation. "We used to think nothing could go the speed of light, but obviously, that's not true, because if you separate these particles far enough, and change the direction of one, the other one will change direction faster than a signal could travel from one to the other at the speed of light."

I felt an obligation to keep Billy on track. "So what's that got to do unicorns, dragons and broomsticks?"

"It doesn't," he said, but he had that distant glaze he sometimes got when a new big idea was forming.

"Mom, you might want to get Billy some paper and a pen. Otherwise he's going to start scratching equations into the dining room table."

Mom got up to do that, while Billy Bobble babbled.

"Not equations. Not yet. Just a… just a model. We think of quarks as particles, right?"

"Uh…" said Mom.

"It's a rhetorical question," I told her, "Best not interrupt him or his brain might explode—like waking up a sleepwalker."

"But what if they aren't particles, but strings."

"Like string theory." Okay, so a little cheerleading on my part might not hurt.

"A little bit, yeah."

Mom handed him the paper and a pen.

"Do you have a rubber band?" Billy asked.

"I think so." Mom shot me an "is he okay" look.

I nodded. He might be suppressing a million things about the events of the week, but it was getting his brain going, which was always good for Billy.

By the time Mom came back with a rubber band, Billy had punched a little hole in a piece of paper. "Okay, imagine for a second, that our universe is entirely contained on a single plane, like this piece of paper."

"A two-dimensional universe."

"Sure, or the hologram projection model, either one. Now, imagine that this rubber band is another universe. If the rubber band universe intersects the paper universe…" He pushed the rubber band through the hole in the paper.

"What would we observe from our paper universe point of view?"

Geometry. Not my strong suit, but I had a pretty good guess. "All we would see is the point of intersection."

"'Point,' singular?"

"No." I was catching on. "The two points where the loop intersects the plane."

Billy turned to Mom, "Mrs. Quinofski, do you remember your geometry?"

"Not a bit of it," but she loved watching us put together a new idea.

"Suzy," Billy said, "in geometry, what is a point?"

"It is the smallest possible thing. More like an idea than an actual object in space."

"Like a quark?"

"Like a quark."

"And if this rubber band is spinning…" He twisted it between his fingers.

"Then both points spin!" That was Mom. She was really getting into this.

"Exactly, Mrs. Q. Suzy, could I destroy one of the points?"

I knew this one. "No, it's not a single point, it's a part of a line. If you destroy one, it's replaced by the next in line."

Billy was on a roll. "If I separate the two points?"

"You're not really separating them," I said. "You're moving the rubber band within the plane."

"What if I smash them together?"

Mom got it this time. "You aren't smashing them together, you're pushing the rubber band outside the paper."

Billy egged her on. "Which would make them…"

"Disappear!" Mom and I said together.

"Exactly!" said Billy.

"Suzy, this quantum physics stuff is fun. Why aren't you more into it?"

"I like my science real, Mom. Besides, microbiologists have a chance to actually make a living beyond a professor's pay."

Billy put the rubber band back through the paper. "One last thing," he said. "If I separate the two particles so far that even light will take a second to travel from one to the other along our piece of paper, then I change the direction of one particle, and the other one changes direction in less than a second, what does that say about the rest of the rubber band?"

He waited for us to answer, but we didn't have a clue.

"It means…" he said, like he was telling a ghost story. "It means that the rest of the rubber band exists outside of our Time, disconnected. In a universe where our laws of physics don't apply."

Don't ask me why, but something about all that conversation sent a chill down my spine.

"Mine, too," said Dr. Weston. "Please tell me he's delusional," she said to Dr. Menaus.

"In the world of quantum physics, everything is delusional, but he presented them a very sound model to explain quarks."

"Did you teach him that?"

"No, it's pretty standard stuff. Except that part about Time being disconnected from Space. I'm going to have to get home and work on the equations to back it up."

They were interrupted by Suzy on the other side of the observation window. "Billy's idea was that something had us locked in the paper universe's time, and that if we could find the key, we could break out to where Time had no meaning at all."

"Is that what you did, Billy?" Menaus asked. "Is that where you've gone?"

Seven

Suzy's Gnome de Plume

SUZY QUINOFSKI TRANSCRIPT - CONTINUED

Billy called me the next morning to say that he would be late to school. He and Peter had to talk to some people about his mom. He was back by lunch time, but he didn't say much. I knew he'd catch me up as we walked home, and I wasn't wrong.

"She's got schizophrenia."

"Oh. I'm so sorry."

"The doctor said her alcoholism probably covered it up for a long time, but…" He drifted off in silent sadness.

"That's good though, because they have medications for that now."

"The doctor said that, too. He also said that we'd have to make sure she stayed on them. Most schizophrenics don't. If they miss once, then their paranoia kicks in. They start hearing voices that tell them the medicine is bad, then it's hard to get them back on it."

"It's going to be tough, huh?"

"It's gonna suck."

We didn't talk at all the rest of the way home. He didn't come in, and I felt so bad for him as he moped across the army base to the trailer park.

I couldn't get it off my mind all night. Schizophrenia. Next to Alzheimer's disease and autism it had to be the saddest of all illnesses. I knew about them pretty well since they had links to microbiology, namely DNA.

Granted, genetics—which is what DNA is all about—isn't the only factor, since there are cases with identical twins where one has the disease and the other doesn't. Environmental factors obviously come into play. There's also something to do with aging, since autism is not apparent until toddler years, schizophrenia until young adulthood, and Alzheimer's until you're really old, and that could mean the answer is in the epigenome... but I digress. The relevant point is that patients in all three cases lose touch with reality.

Billy would say that there is no singular reality. They are losing touch with *our* reality.

Except Alzheimer's patients. They lose their memories.

But from Billy's point of view...

If we slip out of step with linear time...

I had it! I sat bolt upright in bed in the middle of the night with the answer. I threw something on, ran out of the house and didn't stop until I was banging on Billy's window.

"What?" He was obviously asleep.

"Wake up, Billy, I've got it."

"Got what?"

"The key!"

"What key?"

"I know what locks us in time."

That got him up. In an instant he was at the window, wide awake.

"It's DNA."

I waited while Billy got dressed and came out to join me for a walk. Late night walk sessions were becoming nearly as regular as our walks home. Since neither of us had anyone in our families who could understand our school projects, the late night discussions were usually more about scientific issues.

I laid out my hypothesis as we headed toward the trailer park's playground. I told him how schizophrenia, Alzheimer's, and autism patients all lose touch with reality at different stages in their lives and that DNA had to be a major factor.

"So the epigenome, which is like the maintenance crew for DNA, somehow screws up. At least, that's my theory—and a few others', but it doesn't matter. The thing is, it all comes down to DNA." I was getting all excited the way Billy did, but hey, this was my thing like physics was his. We all have our geek-things, I guess.

I let my opening argument sink in, then got to the good stuff. "They also have in common the fact that victims lose touch with reality in one way or another."

"So?"

"So!? You're always talking about multiple realities. What if they aren't so much losing touch with our reality as slipping in and out of an alternate one?"

"They can't… You can't apply quantum mechanics to biology."

"Why not?" I was shocked to be the one defending his crazy ideas.

"Because quantum physics is theoretical. It's not something practical or…"

"Or real?"

I could tell Billy didn't believe he was making this argument. He loved the quantum world. He swore it was real, but here push came to shove and he was backing away from it as fast as he could.

"Okay," he said, "so, it's just a bunch of theories that one day might explain how the Enterprise can travel at warp speed. There, I said it. Are you happy now?"

"No, I'm not. I finally see things your way, and now you can't see it."

"I see fine. But you can't compare Multi-World Theory to Alzheimer's. I mean, Alzheimer's patients lose their memories, it's not like they travel through ti…" He cut himself off.

I could see the dots connecting in his brain. "Now you're getting it."

"If you are shifted into your past, then your nurse taking care of you makes no sense. She must be your child."

"You can remember ten years back like it was yesterday, but not what happened five minutes ago."

"Because for you," he said, "five minutes ago hasn't happened yet!"

"Exactly!"

"And from what you've told me of DNA, most of it is exactly the same for every living thing, only a small part of it defines the species and individual."

"Yeah, so?"

"So?! The key has to have two parts. One defines what Time, or reality, we are all locked into, the other defines the individual who is attached."

"You're saying that all of that non-coding DNA defines our reality..."

"And the rest," he said, "defines who we are."

If our lives were a TV show, they'd have played the dramatic music and cut to commercial as we stood in amazed silence. Practical applications of quantum mechanics in, what Dad calls, the buy-the-groceries-pay-the-bills-real-world are rare. No one had ever related quantum physics theories to brain diseases before. We had a long way to go to prove it, but if we did, it was Nobels for both of us.

Billy summed up. "Alzheimer's affects your DNA in such a way that you experience time—your timeline—out of synch."

"And autistic kids, they seem to not be aware of our reality at all."

"But some things get through. A commonality between our reality and whatever they're experiencing."

"That's why some of them can play like a concert pianist without ever having sat at a piano before."

"Somewhere in one of their realities, they are a concert pianist, so that's how they communicate." Billy was practically running around the park's play area, while I sat in a swing.

"And what about schizophrenics?" I asked.

Billy stopped in his tracks. "Somewhere there's a world where gnomes really do torment my mom."

"Is it just me, or does some of that sound plausible?"

Normally, Detective Reins was full of comments during an interrogation, but he didn't ordinarily have such educated guests. This had been his first interruption in a while—and it wasn't a wise crack, but an honest question.

"Technically, it's not quantum physics," said Dr. Menaus. "The idea that something on a super-subatomic level could affect behavior on the molecular level is… well…" His thought trailed off.

Dr. Weston took over. "There's a lot we don't know about the brain and brain diseases, detective. That makes it easy fodder for a child's imagination."

"If there's so much you don't know," asked Reins, "then how do you know they aren't right?"

"We don't," said the learned doctor of physics.

Eight

Elemental Force

"I worked my butt off isolating introns. Not that anyone in my class appreciated it," Suzy said as an aside to her mother.

"Wait, what?" Something blew past Detective Danner's ears that he didn't quite catch. "What are introns?"

"It's part of your DNA. There's coding DNA, which is what makes you, you and non-coding DNA that we call 'introns.' That's actually most of the volume of the molecule, and no one knows what it does—though, they are discovering more and more about it. Like Billy said, all life forms share much of the same DNA sequences, so these could be the common link to the timeline."

"Can she really isolate introns?" Menaus was getting more impressed with Suzy by the minute.

"Her parents bought her a whole bio lab and set it up in the basement, so anything is possible."

"Good idea," said Reins from behind the camera, "if she gets a scholarship, the thing'll pay for itself ten times over."

In the interrogation room Danner asked Suzy outright, "Did you actually think you could make real magic?"

"I don't know. I guess *I* didn't. Not really. I was just helping my friend chase geese. But, you know, we're kids. What kid doesn't, on some level, believe in magic? That and, it got me a good grade in biology."

SUZY QUINOFSKI TRANSCRIPT - CONTINUED

I gave my presentation to a class full of narcoleptics. I demonstrated how I separated the molecule without breaking it. I showed them the special test tube I had custom ordered. It was glass, a foot and a half long, with a little bulb at the end that held the coding DNA. Down its length were the introns, which looped out and back from the bulb. Of course, the tube was about as thick as a hair, and you couldn't exactly see the molecule, but still, I thought it was pretty cool.

When I told the class that human DNA stretched out would be about a meter long, Martha Maxwell asked, "What's a meter?" Out of all my work, that's my only question.

"Three feet three inches," I said.

"How long is that?"

I gave up.

Mr. Hunter said, "You're getting an A even though I'm not a hundred percent sure what it is you've done. But it sounds very impressive."

Yeah. I was a 12-year-old high school freshman, and still smarter than my teachers.

Billy understood it, though, and that's all that mattered. Of course, he didn't know what to do with it. For the longest time he just poked and prodded the stuff, while I continued to grow and separate more DNA from the ficus tree in my lab. I wanted to build up a stockpile, but Billy kept destroying the tubes—mostly with cold at Oakridge's physics lab. He was sure, if we could get the strands close enough to absolute zero, that when it turned from a solid to a condensate, we'd get results.

We got them all right; a lot of expensive broken glass. Luckily, homework sales were good, so we were well-financed.

One night in my basement lab, Billy was trying to find the introns in the microscope. "Where did they go?"

"DNA is like the string on a yo-yo, it can get all twisted up on itself sometimes."

"Great, DNA is like a string. Particles are like strings."

"If you believe string theory."

"If I could fly a kite, I could solve the riddles of the universe."

"It worked for Ben Franklin. Not Charlie Brown, though. I don't think he ever figured life out."

But Billy didn't hear me. He was Sherlock Holmes

and the game was afoot. He looked up from the microscope with an infinite stare. "What?" I said, careful not to scare his moment away.

"String theory says that the smallest of particles aren't particles at all, but little bundles of energy that wiggle around like strings."

"Yeah, so?"

"So, you remember the rubber band and the paper? Well, instead of us being in a two dimensional universe like the paper, what if it were three, like a box?"

"Then—?"

"Then the rubber band, the other universe that intersects ours, would look like a squiggling loop, and if it were small enough…"

"It would look like a particle."

Billy held one of the special tubes between his fingers, so the introns stretched out behind his hand and the bulb sat in his palm like a ball. "We've been trying to change the DNA molecule, when in fact, all we have to do is push its particles through to the other side of whatever barrier holds them in place." He pushed the bulb through his fingers.

"Okay, great. How do we do that?"

"No idea."

"Wow," was all Menaus could say.

"Doctor–"

"No, no," he scolded, "Anton."

Cassie skipped the name issue. "I brought you here to help me prove they're delusional, not right."

"Sorry, but this idea of strings being looped through another dimensional barrier is brilliant." He started writing up equations on a notepad. "Why didn't Billy come to me with this?"

Probably because he didn't trust you any more than I do, Weston thought. Menaus wouldn't have been the first professor to publish one of his student's ideas, but he might have been the first one to steal from 12-year-olds. Good thing she was here to witness their work.

With that thought, Weston realized she was beginning to buy into the delusion herself. "Billy Bobble did not make a magic wand."

"What?" asked Menaus, distracted by his notes—and Weston blushed with the realization that she'd said that out loud.

"Nothing." She went back to listening to Suzy.

SUZY QUINOFSKI TRANSCRIPT - CONTINUED

They were talking about auras—the coven, I mean—in study hall. As usual, Billy couldn't handle the balance between drooling over the girls and wanting to set the science straight.

Sonni was talking about a guy she had a crush on. "I could totally see his aura was dark blue with red shimmers."

He couldn't leave it alone. "Actually…"

Linda said what I was thinking. "Don't start with your science crap, Billy."

"I was going to say—"

But it was Lisa's turn to talk. "Aura's are real."

Then Mary's. "They've photographed them and everything."

Then it was Billy's turn to shut up, but did he? Of course not. "That's Kirlian photography. It would give an aura to a rock."

Then Linda: "What if a rock has an aura?"

"I thought only living things have them." Oh, Billy slipped in out of turn. No matter, the witches didn't miss a beat.

Sonni. "They do."

Lisa. "That doesn't mean the rock doesn't have life on it."

And Mary bringing up the rear. "Yeah."

Once again, Billy blew the chance to say "fine" and let the subject drop. "With Kirlian photography you run a charge through the film plate, then when you put something on it—alive or not—it reflects the charge."

Now Linda. "That doesn't mean auras aren't real."

But Billy's daydream stopped the flow. "Anything," he said, then to me, "The reflection is dependent upon the conductivity..."

Before he could finish that thought, someone came into study hall and handed Mrs. Nelson a note. "Billy," she said after reading it.

I saw Peter waiting for him. He mouthed "Mom" to Billy, who quickly took his things and left.

"Your boyfriend needs to lighten up," said Linda once Billy was out the door.

It took me a second to realize she was talking to me. "He's not my boyfriend."

"Come on," said Mary.

"Everybody knows you two are together," said Sonni.
"You were born for each other," said Lisa.
"Yeah," added Linda, "and you've both got it made."
"Wait. What?" I said.
"You're both brainiacs," said Mary.
"Totally smart," said Sonni.
"You know, like, everything," said Lisa.

"Really?" I don't know what it was, but something about them set me off. Maybe it was the stress of Billy's ordeal, or being a 12-year-old girl in a 14-through-18-year-old's world. Or maybe it was something else that I didn't want to think about, but they got under my skin. "That's what you think, that we know everything? Well, if we know so much, why can't I put together an outfit that doesn't make me look like a dweeb? Why can't I get anyone besides Billy to notice my existence? Why can't Billy get you girls to like him?"

That shut them up.

"Something I do know," I told them, "there's more to life than what they put in tests or teach us in school. So Billy and I do well in those things, great. Goody for us, but do you ever see us at dances or parties? You have your spells to try to control your world, to make your wishes come true; well, you know what? Everyone has wishes. Everyone has dreams, or nightmares, that they would like to come true or disappear."

I thought about Billy and his driving desire to make his wand. I thought about the nightmares in his life. How his wishes: to help his mom—or maybe get away from her—to get to know his dad, to get out of the trailerhood. I thought of all of Billy's wishes and realized they'd become mine as well. That might have been the thing I didn't want to think about.

"Everyone needs a little magic in their life," I said, but I think they'd stopped listening.

Billy was waiting for me in front of the school for our walk home.

"I've got the answer," he said, before so much as a "hi, how are you?"

"Billy? How's your mom?"

"What? Oh, yeah, she's fine. She'll be home tomorrow. They gave her electroshock therapy."

"Billy!? That's serious."

"So am I."

Okay, I'm not a psychiatrist or anything, but I know there's a syndrome for how much he was not talking about his mother.

"I don't know what took me so long to see it," he said as we walked. "It has to be one of the four fundamental forces."

"Billy…" I didn't think it was the right time to be playing around with our experiment.

"I guess us quantum guys are so used to tossing out standard physics that we forget about the basics."

"Billy don't you want to talk–?"

"No!" He stopped walking, but couldn't bring himself to look at me. "I don't want to talk about it." After a brief second, he started walking again with, "And I don't want to mess around with Strong Force. I mean, we want to shift the atoms, not split them, right?"

I didn't say a thing. I just kept pace and stared him down as best as I could without tripping.

"Right?" he asked again.

I stopped. He stopped. I still didn't say anything.

"Suzy." He finally made eye contact, and I could see his were red and wet. "I can't handle the real world right now, so I need you to be my friend and not press me about Mom, okay?"

"How do I know that I'm not being a better friend by holding your feet to the fire?"

Billy thought about this for a while, then said, "We don't want to split the atoms, we just want to push them out of our dimension, right?"

I set my jaw, crossed my arms and in every way that I could think of indicated my displeasure with his decision, then said, "Right." He started walking again. "But we're coming back to this," I said before I caught up to him.

He ignored that. "So Strong Force is out."

"Right," I said. I had a vague memory from a science show on TV that Strong Force is what holds atoms together and is responsible for the E in $E= mc^2$ aka nuclear explosions, so I was glad we weren't dealing with that.

"Weak Force doesn't apply because we're not dealing with radioactivity."

"Thank God for that."

"Gravity."

"Gravity's just a theory," I said. One of our favorite jokes—even if it is true. I was hoping for a witty retort, but he stayed on track.

"Gravity obviously doesn't apply."

He had pushed my rudimentary knowledge of physics to the limit. "What does that leave?"

He stopped again. "Electromagnetism."

"Electricity?" I asked. Billy's lips pursed so tight that the lower half of his face turned yellow and white from the pressure. "Billy…"

"I got the idea when they rebooted Mom's brain."

"Maybe we should stop this, Billy."

It was seven o'clock at night. He'd been working in my basement lab since we got home from school. From his discussion with the Coven, he'd thought to set up a Kirlian photography rig using a car battery and Dad's old scanner/copier. He wired the whole thing into his laptop so he could see real time Kirlian Video. Turns out, the coding DNA in the tiny bulb at the bottom of my glass tubes had a different electromagnetic signature than the non-coding down the length.

"No, no. You were right."

"*I* was right? About what?"

"The brain and DNA. It… it's… Awareness! That's the word I'm looking for. Some people are more aware than others. So what do we do to them? We shock them back to our reality so they make sense to us—instead of making sense to themselves, you know?"

Billy was sweating up a storm. He hadn't sat down, relaxed, taken a break, or stopped moving, even when he was standing still, for hours. Mom got home around six. I filled her in on what was going on—about Billy's mother and how he worked on this impossible idea of making magic instead of dealing with the real world. Mom took to worrying. She pulled her wife-of-the-general strings and got the company doctor on the phone.

"Is he suicidal?" Mom asked me, relaying the question from the other end of the conversation.

"I don't think so," I said.

"We don't think so," Mom told the doctor. Then she asked me, "Is he dangerous?"

"No more than usual." Sure, he had a bunch of wire and power tools—but that was typical for Billy.

"We don't think he's dangerous. I mean, he's working on an experiment with a car battery and …?"

"Intron-isolated DNA."

"And stuff," she told the doctor, "but that's not unusual for Billy." The doctor must have asked something personal, because Mom got all flustered. "No, no. He would never. No." Then she asked me, "Billy doesn't take drugs does he?"

"Mom! … Billy."

"Right," she said, completely understanding what I meant. She started to go back to the phone, then asked me. "Do you do drugs?"

"Mom! … Me."

"Right. I love you, honey, you don't ever need to… You can always come to us."

"Mom. The doctor."

"Oh, sorry," she said into the phone. "Definitely no drugs." She then went through several "yeah, okays" before thanking him and hanging up. "He said Billy was having a natural reaction to his situation, and that we should make sure he doesn't do anything radical. Eventually, he'll run out of steam, sleep, and we can help him deal with his issues after he's past this initial... whatever he said it was."

"Acute mania," I said.

"That's it, yes. If he doesn't come out of it, then it might become an issue."

With that, she came down to the basement with me to ask if Billy wanted to stop and eat.

"Stop? No. Eat? Yes," he said.

Thirty minutes later, Mom brought down dinner. Billy thanked her and ate enough to keep a hummingbird stuffed for five minutes, all while still working on his idea.

By ten o'clock he'd stripped thin copper wires from an old toy robot that he'd left at my house years ago and wrapped them around the glass tube. He would re-arrange the wires, check the magnetic field, then tell me to get set. I'd put on my lab goggles and stand back—even though I knew the whole thing was stupid. Billy would do the same, but with insane enthusiasm, and press a button to run the car battery current through the wires.

Nothing happened.

So Billy would check the playback on the Kirlian video, and try again. This went on until one in the morning.

"Billy, please. Can we give it a rest until tomorrow?"

"Just… just… just…" he kept saying as he ran around adjusting things. "Just one more try."

"That's what you said fifty tries ago."

"I know, but I feel good about this one."

"That's what you said about the last seventy tries."

Billy was now at the firing button. "Just put your goggles on."

"Why? Nothing's going to happen."

"Lab rules. Your father made us promise."

I put on my goggles and schlepped over to my spot across the room. Billy hit the power button and WHAM! An explosion ripped through the basement, knocking me and Billy on our butts, out cold—literally, freezing cold.

Nine

I Wood If I Could

SUZY QUINOFSKI TRANSCRIPT - CONTINUED

You know how when you wreck your bike, or maybe you're in a car accident, things go in slow motion? Maybe you only remember them that way, I don't know, but that's the way I have the explosion in my head. I can still see the cold, brilliant, white light shatter the glass tube. A shockwave flashed through the room. When it struck me, I thought my chest would crash through my back. Next thing I know, I'm flying through the air. I don't remember hitting the ground, or the wall, or whatever gave me a big bruise on my shoulder. I do remember feeling like I'd walked into a super cold freezer.

I came to in a pile of debris with Billy moaning into consciousness next to me. Before I could realize that my breath was visible in the chill, and what that might mean on a hot spring night, Mom came running down the stairs.

"What happened? Are you two all right?"

"I'm okay," I said. "Billy?"

"Wow! Did you see that?"

"Saw it. Heard it. Felt it," I said. "Mostly felt it."

Mom was still trying to catch up. "What on earth is going on?"

"Sorry, Mrs. Q," said Billy, "that was completely unexpected."

"Are you both all right?"

"I'm fine, I think," said Billy as he took an inventory of his muscles and bones. "Suzy? You okay, too?"

"I appear to be."

"No, you don't," said Mom. "What's that sticking out of your face?"

I reached up to find a shard of plastic imbedded in my goggles. I took them off. "Nothing, Mom, see. Had my goggles on."

"Thank goodness for that. Did either of you lose consciousness?"

Mom knew the answer from the way Billy and I looked at each other. "I'm calling Dr. Mead," she said. Halfway up the stairs to our land-line phone she stopped. "And your father."

Oh, great. "Mom! Dad's in, like, Iran or some crazy place."

But she was unstoppable. "I don't care," she shouted from the top of the steps.

Billy looked like a guilty puppy. "Are you going to get in trouble?"

"Are you kidding? Dad's a general. He likes stuff that blows up."

Billy's guilt left him in a flash. "Good, because we have to work fast." He started inspecting the mess.

"What are you talking about?"

Billy put his hand on a steaming aluminum next to me that had once been a centrifuge. "It's cold. Everything here is cold."

"So? It was an endothermic reaction." That was a lesson Billy had given with a chemical ice pack in first grade.

"You ever hear of an endothermic explosion?"

"I don't know. You're the physics geek."

Billy paced around while I started checking out the explosion site myself. Billy talked out his thoughts. "I suppose cold explosions can happen, but they'd be rare, and definitely not as big as what we just saw." I was only half-listening. Something was wrong about the basement, but I couldn't figure it out.

"And I can hear," Billy blurted out. "Can you hear?"

"I wish I couldn't."

"An explosion that big in a cinder block room—our ears should be bleeding. We should be deaf."

"That's true. It wasn't like any explosion I've ever seen—and I've seen a few with Dad."

"I suppose we could have blown out a window, that would explain the cold."

That's when I realized, "Billy, it's Spring. It's 80 degrees outside."

He inspected the steam coming off the rubble and wafted a little bit of it under his nose. "Water vapor," he said.

I picked up an empty can of soda that had been sitting

in the sink for hours. "It's freezing cold." I felt the upturned porcelain. "The sink is, too."

"What kind of explosion doesn't make as much noise as it should and freezes everything in its path?" Billy strolled around the rubble, but was looking for answers in his head. "What could flash-freeze an entire room?"

That's when I noticed, "There's nothing wrong with the table."

"Well, the blast could have pushed on the table straight down with an even pressure, wouldn't have affected it. Stranger things have happened in explosions."

Neither one of us said anything else until he blurted out, "That's it!"

"What?" He'd startled me.

"What can flash-freeze an entire room?"

"If you name a comic book character, I'm going to kill you."

"No. Bose-Einstein Condensate. It's not a gas, liquid, solid, or plasma. It's matter and/or energy at zero degrees Kelvin, so an eruption might not create the concussion of a normal explosion. And nothing gets that cold, anywhere. Ever. But I'll bet you that's what's in the barrier between our timeline and the quantum universe."

"So your cold idea wasn't such a bad one after all, huh?"

"Yeah, except instead of us freezing it, it froze us."

Something was still funky about the table. I touched it. "It's not cold." Then I pointed out a wooden test tube holder sitting exactly where I'd left it on the table, but all the tubes in it had been destroyed.

"Uh... I've got nothing," said Billy about my observation.

I checked the holder. It wasn't cold. We both roamed around the room trying to put the pieces of the puzzle together and got the "ah-ha" at the same time. "Wood," we said to each other.

Anything and everything made of wood in the basement was intact, no damage, not cold. Everything else was blasted and pumping out icy cold water vapor.

Billy said what I was thinking. "We're definitely on to something completely different."

"No fart jokes, okay?"

Dr. Mead had been my doctor for as long as I can remember, but this was the first time he'd made a house call. Well, sort of. The base bomb squad was in the basement, so we were out in the yard for our own protection. He was a funny old guy. He'd put his two index fingers out for Billy and I to squeeze. Once we got over laughing about "pull my finger," we did. Equal strength in both hands. No paralysis. Good.

Dr. Mead turned his pen light on Billy. "Got a headache?"

"A little bit," said Billy.

"Well, relax," said the doctor, "shining this light in your eyes will make it much worse."

We giggled a little while he checked out Billy's pupil response, then made him put his arms out like an airplane.

"Are we going to have to get CT scans?" I asked.

He ignored me. "Billy, try to keep me from pushing your hands down."

We were getting neurological exams. My favorite! "Of

course," I said, "our age and the lack of a massive trauma counter-indicate brain imagining, but still. I'd love to see my own brain."

Dr. Mead finally answered me, but kept his eyes on Billy. "Maybe your mother can bring you by sometime and I can run one for you."

"Really?" That would be so friggin' cool!

"You're the boss's daughter," he said. "Might as well take advantage of it." He then got serious. "Billy. Earlier this evening Mrs. Quinofski called me. She was worried that you might be upset about something."

"Oh, yeah." Billy bowed his head. "I was. Still am."

"Do you remember what it is you're upset about?"

I chimed in. "That's a memory check. Diagnostic tool. Very good, Dr. Mead."

"Suzy," he said, then put his finger to his lips.

Yeah... I can get a little out of control around practical biology, especially as it deals with the brain. "Sorry."

He gave me an it's-okay nod, then said, "Billy?"

"Yeah, I remember. We just found out my mom has schizophrenia and she had shock therapy."

"And that upset you." Dr. Mead had the smoothest tone to his voice. If I didn't already have two grandfathers, I'd want him to be one.

"I guess, yeah."

"Enough to maybe... I don't know... blow something up?"

He was way off base. I had to jump in. "Oh no! No, Dr. Mead, nothing like that."

Billy came to his own defense, too. "She's right, Doctor. This was an accident."

"The kids aren't lying." I turned to see what baritone just joined the conversation, and let me just say... wow! He was a hunk of a special ops Captain, dressed in a cross between military fatigues and a fireman's outfit. I quickly glanced around to share this eye-candy moment, but the only other woman not in uniform was Mom. Ew.

"This is a curious case," said Captain Hot. "I'm sure we'll study it for a long time, but it appears that hydrogen gas escaped from the car battery, which is normal. It must have built up. We're not exactly sure where, but apparently it found some spark of ignition, and boom." Billy's eyes darted toward me. I wanted to believe the new love of my life, but Billy's look was right. That wasn't what happened.

"Or pop," said the Captain. He couldn't see our skeptic looks in the dark. "Not a lot of energy in hydrogen, which is why there's no fire. We even found water droplets."

"$H_2 0$," said Billy.

He had a tone only I could notice. It was his you-must-be-right hint of sarcasm; his way of telling me we'd keep our mouths shut.

"Exactly," said the Captain. Why is it no one expects a 12-year-old to know anything about basic chemistry? "Hydrogen plus oxygen and a spark. Boom, water."

"That must have been it, huh?" Billy was right on the edge of incredulous.

He gave Billy a hard stare. "Just a first guess." Apparently, Captain Hot wasn't as dumb as most women would want him to be. He then softened for Dr. Mead. "But definitely an accident."

That's when Mom ruined the whole thing by speaking up. "Captain, are you sure?"

"Ms. Quinofski..." He should have been saying that to me. "I'm on your husband's speed dial. And the FBI come to us to train."

"Cool."

Billy could shut-up, too. This was between me and my Captain.

"No, not cool," said my future husband. "We don't like making house calls, okay?"

Wait, what?

"Sorry about that," said Billy.

"That's okay," said Mom with a lilt in her voice. "Come back anytime."

MOM!

"Go away."

That was Peter's bark anytime his little brother was within ten feet of him.

By the time we'd gotten the run down on our minor concussions and said good-bye to the bomb squad, it was nearly dawn. Exhaustion finally caught up with Billy. He barely made it to the guest bed before passing out. Luckily it was Saturday, so we both slept until almost noon. After a quick bite, we headed over to Billy's to see if we could get his brother's help. Although Billy and I possessed many skills, carpentry wasn't one of them. Peter had a genius for anything to do with tools, so that's how we ended up knocking on his bedroom door that Saturday afternoon.

"Peter, it's me," said Billy.

"All the more reason for you to go away."

"We need your help."

Peter finally opened his door, letting out a cloud of smoke. "That's an understatement." Apparently, he didn't come out to talk to us, as he pushed his way down the path of junk toward the kitchen. "What do you two neophyte Newtons need from me? A ride to the mall?"

"No," said Billy. We tagged along behind him like puppy dogs. "We need your carpentry skills."

Peter opened a bag of cookies and started pumping them into his face. While he carried them to his shop outside, Billy explained about his idea to make real, scientific magic, and the glass tube with the separated DNA, and finally, the events of last night.

"You blew up Suzy's basement? Cool. Didn't think you two geeks had it in you." By this time, Peter was uncovering his car.

"Oh, you'd be surprised," said Billy.

"No, I wouldn't."

Before this broke down into a family spat, I jumped to the point. "We need a wooden container, about a foot and a half long, to hold the introns."

"And a battery," added Billy.

"Introns?" asked Peter. "What are those?"

Finally, he was showing some interest. "Well," I started, "through ions of evolution—"

He cut me off. "Eh. Forget that. How big are they? How much do they weigh?"

"Stretched out like that they're about 16 inches long," I said, "and their diameter is about a thousand times less than a human hair. As for weight—"

He interrupted me again. "Never mind about the weight. How big of a battery?"

Billy took that question. "Well, a 12-volt car battery nearly blew up Suzy's basement, so we're thinking a double-A."

Peter summed up, "You want a piece of wood that's about 18 inches long that can hold something like a strand of hair and tiny wires running along it that connect to a double-A battery so you can try to make magic?"

"Yeah," said Billy. "Oh, and a power switch, or button on the side would be good, too."

"You guys are idiots." Peter put the car cover in his trunk and walked toward the driver's door.

That left us standing there mystified. How could he say that? The whole town knew that we were a lot of things, but "idiots" wasn't one of them. But what could we say? Peter had to help us. We had nowhere else to turn.

As we were about to get on our knees and beg, he said, "Come on, geniuses, let's go shopping."

Our trip in Peter's car landed us at the mall.

"What are we doing here?" asked Billy. "Don't we need lumber?"

"I really don't get why people think you're so smart," said Peter as he ignored us once again and walked toward the stores.

We followed.

Where Billy and I could have danced naked down the halls of this modern marketplace without being noticed,

Peter got a smile and wave from every teenager or young adult there. I heard soprano "Hi, Peeeeters" from the girls, and "Pete!" or "Pe-tEE!" baritones from the guys. Peter gave a head toss of recognition to each of them, fidgeted with a toothpick that had somehow found its way into his mouth, and sauntered a bee-line to a gift store.

He ignored all of the day glow posters, pushed past the dirty playing cards and drinking glasses, and went right to the magic tricks section. "Take your pick," he said, indicating a wall full of authentic Harry Potter wands.

"Peter!" said Billy, fuming. "We're serious."

"So am I," he said. "Take a look."

Sure enough, they were all about 18 inches long, made of wood, and perfect for holding the elongated introns, with coding DNA at the base, right in front of a double-A battery in the handle.

"All I have to do is split it along the length," said Peter, "which won't be easy, then rout the insides, and if I'm really good, I can drill tiny holes for you to wrap your wires around. Then you're set. You'll have yourself a real magic wand."

"We've got a problem."

It was a day after our trip to the mall. I'd done a more careful inventory of the damage to my lab and had to give Billy the bad news. "The explosion destroyed all of my DNA samples."

"There has to be some left in the rubble," said Billy, like I could find strands of DNA splattered on the walls.

"They were blown to smithereens."

"So? Even smithereens have mass. How do you think the FBI finds mad bombers?"

"I'm not the FBI."

He must have seen the steam coming out of my ears, because he backed off. "Okay, you're right. I'm sorry."

"It'll take me months to grow and separate more, and I'm not even sure I can with all my equipment blown up."

"It's not a problem," said Billy. He was walking the fine line between optimist and idiot. "I still have the DNA you grew from my cheek swab frozen at home. We'll use that and steal time at the Oakridge lab like we used to."

Okay, so maybe he did have some pragmatism left, but still, "Will it work using your DNA?"

"Sure, why not? If our theory is right, any DNA should do."

"That was our big mistake," Suzy told Detective Danner. "I hope it wasn't a fatal one."

"We all do, Suzy," said Danner.

Behind the observation mirror, Dr. Weston asked Dr. Menaus the question she hoped she wouldn't have to ask from the moment she called him. "I brought you here because I thought Suzy might be delusional—and that still may be the case—but clearly she'd be buying into Billy's delusions, like their own little two-person cult. So my question is; is Billy living in a fantasy world, or does any of this make sense?"

Dr. Menaus didn't pause in writing the algebraic notes he had been scribbling for the past several minutes. "In quantum physics you have models, and you have math. A model without the math to back it up is just, I don't know, wild imagination. But Billy's taken this a step further, into a practical application. There are very few of those in quantum physics."

"Look, Dr. Menaus—"

"Anton."

"—the academic stuff is all fine and dandy, but I'm worried there might be a sick kid out there who set off a bomb at his school."

"That's not what you should be worried about. You'd better *hope* you have a sick kid who set off a bomb at his school."

"What?" Weston's list of people who might be crazy was growing in her mind.

Menaus finally looked up from his notes. "Do you know about the Hadron Super Collider in Switzerland?"

Weston had heard of it. "Is that the thing that could make a black hole and destroy the world?"

"Well, that won't happen, but it is one of those practical applications and it is very dangerous. If the super conductors quench, the beam could cut a hundred meter hole through anything in its path."

The tiny observation room fell silent until Cassie drummed up some confidence. "But that's not going to happen."

"You want another example of applied quantum mechanics in the practical world? How about the atomic bomb?"

Cassie couldn't believe what she was hearing. "Are you telling me…?"

"This kid has done something no adult physicist would ever do. He got the math wrong on purpose." He held up the notepad he'd been writing on. "If he can turn these equations into reality, Billy Bobble could destroy the universe."

Ten

The Big Bang

SUZY QUINOFSKI TRANSCRIPT - CONTINUED

Peter texted Billy during school to say that the wand was ready, so we headed over after class.

As soon as we hit the driveway Peter was after us. "Come take a look." His shop was a covered carport off the side of their trailer. "I had to get all kinds of special tools for this, and I went through about a dozen wands before I got it right, so you geeks better like it."

On his work table was the wand—split length-wise—in a set of vise grips. It had been hollowed out in the middle, with an inner groove for the DNA and an outer one for wires. It was very impressive.

Billy made a visual inspection without touching it. "Wow, this is great."

"See. You've got a place for the DNA stuff, then you can wrap wires around the inner part without smushing the insides."

"Excellent, really," said Billy. "You are a great carpenter. Who knew?"

"Well, you hide from Mom in your room with your books and computer. I do it out here with my car and tools."

Billy looked away, then down at his shoes. "Yeah."

"I've got a few wands left over," said Peter. "Some split some not—if you want those, too."

"Oh, um, maybe. I don't know."

"I'll hang onto to them, just in case."

"Yeah, okay." Billy moved his arms around like he didn't know what to do with them. Crossed them. Put his hands in his back pockets. It was like he didn't know what to do with himself in a regular conversation with his big brother. "Maybe, just in case." I think he was trying to act cool, and as usual, failed.

The loving family moment turned into an awkward male bonding silence until Peter took the two halves of the wand and handed them to Billy. "There you go. One magic wand, ready for loading."

Billy held the wood as if it were butterfly wings. "Thanks," he said, "You know, for doing this."

"Thanks for asking."

If this piece of wood did nothing else, it had already worked magic on Billy and Peter's relationship.

After that, it wasn't long before I worked Billy's DNA into position inside the wand, and Billy had his wires wrapped and ready to go.

"How do you know it's wired right?" I asked. "It took a million tries with the ficus tree sample."

"Yeah, well, I wasn't randomly making changes, was I? I'm trying to implode the magnetic field the way a nuclear trigger implodes the fission material, thus pushing the particles—"

"Okay, forget I asked." It was getting late, or rather early on a Friday morning. I knew Billy was tired because he just said "thus," even though I'd told him a thousand times that no one says that in casual conversation. "Finish what you're doing so we can get some sleep."

Billy put wood glue around the edges and folded the two pieces together. "There we have it. One magic wand."

"Or one very high tech stick that does nothing. How are we going to test it?"

"I was thinking about that. Your house might hold up to another explosion, but…"

"The house, maybe. Mom, definitely not."

"So we'll test it after school on the football field. Plenty of room there for a harmless endoplasmic eruption of super cold Bose-Einstein Condensation."

"If that's what it is."

"If we can even get this thing to work," he said, taking the wand out of the vise grips.

"Where are you taking it?"

He put it in his jacket pocket and headed toward the backdoor. "Home. I want Peter to smooth out the seam."

"Be careful."

"Don't worry, I won't put the battery in until we're done, and I won't test it without you." With that, he left, shouting as he went, "See you at lunch tomorrow."

I started to go to bed, but then remembered I hadn't watered my plants since we cleaned up after the explosion. I filled my jug, watered the small ones, then went to do the ficus tree, but it wasn't there. I looked around for a while before I remembered that the blast must have gotten it, so I put the jug in the sink and went to bed.

But I couldn't sleep. Something was bugging me that I couldn't put my finger on. Just before dawn I realized what it was. Did I clean up the ficus tree after the explosion? I couldn't remember seeing any of it. Not a leaf, twig, bit of dirt, anything. If it wasn't blown up, and it wasn't in the lab, where was it?

Mom stuck her head out of her bedroom window when the noise of my digging in the trashcans woke her up. "Honey, what are you doing?"

"Even smithereens have mass, Mom."

"What?"

"My ficus tree is gone."

"Out of all of that expensive equipment, you're worried about your tree?"

"That stuff's not gone, Mom. It's here, destroyed. The ficus tree is *gone*."

"What's the difference?"

"The difference is… I have to call Billy."

"Honey, no you don't. It's five thirty in the morning. Whatever you have to tell him can wait."

I thought about that. He did promise not to test it

without me, so I could tell him at lunch. Or I could call him on my way to school in the morning.

I shouldn't have waited, though. I should have called him right when I knew.

I got voice mail.

"Billy, listen. I couldn't find my ficus tree anywhere. Not a single smithereen. And since that was the source of the DNA, well, just don't do anything until we talk at lunch."

"Problem?" Mom asked. It was Friday. I had an open first period, so Mom drove me to school to give me extra time to sleep. Funny how, when you can't sleep all night, you suddenly find you can't wake up in the morning.

"No. Shouldn't be," I said, but I was worried. Billy was not the type of guy that could resist whipping out his wand if he thought it might impress someone. I had little faith in his promise not to test it without me.

At lunch, my fears were confirmed.

The knot in my stomach started when I noticed Billy wasn't sitting in his usual spot. It tightened when I saw a crowd gathering around the Coven's area of the courtyard. There was laughter. The cruel kind of laughter that only kids and bullies are capable of.

I started to run toward the crowd.

"Go on, Billy, whip it out for us."

Linda. She would murder him, if for no other reason than to vent her own social stigma on him. Tearing Billy to pieces would make her feel whole, and when it came to Linda, Billy had no defenses.

"Billy, don't!" I shouted, but no one could hear me. If I could have just made eye contact, but Billy was staring blankly forward with his jaw set. I knew that look. It was his "I'll show you" face.

Slowly, without breaking his stare, he pulled out the store-bought Harry Potter wand that only a child or a crazy fan could appreciate. A lot of the kids recognized it because they probably had one at home. That only added to the ridiculousness of Billy drawing the stick as if were a delicate instrument.

The laughter showed no sign of stopping. Kids were holding their sides or rolling on the ground. Sonni and Mary had to lean on each other for support as tears of unending laughter rolled down their faces. Linda managed to get out between rolling chortles, "Billy Bobble made a magic wand. That's hilarious!"

As everyone fell away laughing, it left only me and Billy standing upright. I caught his eye before he did it. He smiled the saddest, weakest smile I'd ever seen. I guess it was an attempt to say, "Hey, I can laugh this off," but we both knew he couldn't. I think the tears on my cheeks were his final undoing. Pity, from me, his best friend. His humiliation was complete.

That's when he pushed the button.

That's when the cold white flash of light exploded in the courtyard. The kids around Billy toppled like dominoes. There was a loud clap of thunder and dirt from the courtyard flew up to occupy the space where Billy once stood. When the shockwave passed over me—still white and cold—it smelled like Billy. That's when I knew he was gone.

END OF TRANSCRIPT

"I guess you know the rest," Suzy said. Her story had exhausted her, but she was glad to have the whole thing out and on the record. Now maybe they would understand and start looking for Billy.

"That's your story?" asked Detective Danner.

"Final answer," said Suzy.

"Okay."

"It's the truth."

Danner asked Mrs. Quinofski, "Could I see you outside?"

She checked in with her daughter. "Will you be—?"

"I'm fine, Mom. Let's get this over with so we can go home."

With a nod to the observation window, he led Janice into the hall.

Suzy stared at the two-way mirror and wondered if someone was still on the other side. If she was still being recorded. Probably. Didn't matter. What was she going to do in an empty interrogation room?

Then she studied her reflection, hardly recognizing the girl that stared back. Dirt splotched every inch of her, especially her hands up to her elbows. After the explosion she charged the area, desperate to find Billy or any sign of where he might have gone. Her eyes were red from tears and black from lack of sleep.

"What have I become?" she asked herself.

The mirror was set in a metal frame that connected it to the cinderblock wall. Countless fellow inmates had etched graffiti into the thin paint. As if presented as an answer to her question, she recognized a name.

She got out of the chair for the first time in hours to run her fingers over the letters.

P. Bobble.

"Peter. Where's your little brother?" Her eyes filled with tears. "Where are you, B. Bobble?"

Part Two

A World With Magic

Eleven

Run for Your Life

"**D**ON'T SAY ANYTHING." Janice whispered in her daughter's ear when she hugged her good-bye in the interrogation room. "Your Dad's on his way, and I'm getting an attorney."

"They don't believe me, do they?"

"It doesn't matter what they believe, honey. It matters what they can prove." One day in the criminal justice system and Mrs. Quinofski was talking like a mob boss. "Wait here. They want me to do some paperwork. I'll be back as soon as I can to take you home."

A kiss and a tight hug, and Suzy was once again alone in her empty room.

Dr. Menaus didn't join the other adults in the hall to discuss Suzy's fate. He was too busy scribbling equations on a notepad. When the silence finally got his attention, he looked up to be startled by Suzy nearly standing on top of him. After his initial start, he remembered she was on the other side of a thick piece of glass.

"Where are you B. Bobble?" she asked.

"Where indeed?" said Menaus out loud to no one.

Suzy's mother came back in, so Menaus returned to his work. T = c/0. Time equals the speed of light divided by zero, an impossible equation, but according to his figures, that's exactly where Billy was. Somewhere impossible.

Suzy's mother left after a short conversation. Menaus stared through the glass at nothing in particular, trying to get his head around the story he'd just heard. Facts, supporting a theory, applied by children. What was real science and what was just wishful thinking? He wasn't sure.

Shortly after that, all of his questions were answered. From nowhere Billy appeared.

He was preceded by a loud crack and a flash of cold white light that made Suzy jump nearly to the ceiling.

"Billy!"

"I'm… so… cold…" he managed to say.

"Where have you been?"

"Don't know. It was horrible. Where am I now?"

"You're in a police station."

"Oh. That's an improvement."

"How did you get here? What happened?"

"I don't know. It was bad. Um… um…"

"You were at school."

"Right. Everyone was laughing at me."

"They aren't laughing now. We're in trouble."

"I just wanted to disappear. That's all I was thinking. I wanted to disappear off the face of the earth."

"Well, you succeeded. Where did you go?"

"Nowhere. I was nowhere at all. I was in … nothingness."

She saw so much fear in him that it scared her. She steered away from the question. "How did you get here?"

"I wanted to go home," said Billy. "I thought about home and what that meant to me."

"And you landed here? You have a freaky sense of home, Bobble." Her levity helped them both.

A shout came from down the hall. "Hey! What's going on in there?"

"Billy, we are in so much trouble. You have no idea," Suzy said, as Billy dragged himself up off the floor "They think we faked it. That we blew-up the courtyard at school as part of a prank."

"Suzy, is someone in there with you?"

"They think we're juvenile delinquents," said Suzy.

Billy's mind spun. Another Bobble juvie. No one would be surprised.

"They don't believe us, Billy!"

"Yeah? Well, believe this!" If he was going to be a delinquent, he was determined to be a good one. So much so, that he would risk the horrors of magic one more time. He jammed a chair under the doorknob, raised his wand with one hand and grabbed Suzy with the other. "Think about your lab," he told her.

"What?"

"Just do it! I have a hypothesis."

"A *hypothesis*!? Billy, this is no time for guessing!"

"Think hard about your lab. Like your life depends on it."

"Does it?"

"It might."

Suzy squeezed her eyes shut and did as she was told. Billy thought about Suzy's lab, and pushed the button.

The explosion knocked Menaus off his chair. He scrambled to his feet to see a ficus tree standing where the two kids once were.

"What's going on in there?" came a voice from outside the interrogation room door.

Menaus watched the door struggle against the chair. He only had a few seconds before they'd figure out to join him in the observation room. His eyes shot to the video camera. It was recording.

He hit rewind.

How long had they been together? he thought. *How far back do I go?* He didn't have time to be precise, so he did what he could, hit record, then sat as far away from it as possible with his back to the glass.

When the detectives stormed in, they went straight to the two-way mirror, not noticing the scientist, buried in his notes and discreetly putting in his music headphones.

"What is she playing at?" asked Danner.

His partner was just as stymied. "How did she get that tree in there?"

Danner finally noticed they weren't alone. As he'd never met the professor, he tossed his head in his direction for Reins's benefit.

"Hey, professor," said Reins.

No response.

Reins waved. "Professor?"

Menaus pulled a plug out of one ear. Some song from the 1960s blared out as if a tiny party was going on inside his head. "I'm sorry. You talking to me?"

"Yeah. You didn't see..." he pointed toward the interrogation room as his voice trailed off. If the man had seen anything no further words would have been needed. "You didn't hear that explosion?"

Menaus indicated his headphones. "Sorry. Little trick I learned from Thomas Edison. He was mostly deaf, so he enjoyed working undisturbed."

"Suzy?"

"Billy?"

"Where are you?"

"I'm right here. Where are you?"

"I think the question is, where are *we*?"

"I can't see anything," said Suzy.

"See, hear, taste, touch, smell—pretty much all of my five senses are toast."

"You can hear me, stupid."

"Oh, yeah..." Billy ran his mind over that for a second

then offered, "Unless we're talking telepathically."

Suzy was going to say that was dumb, but thought better of it. Then she wondered if Billy knew what she just thought. Then Billy didn't seem to be around at all. Suzy panicked for what could have been five seconds or five years. She had no way of knowing.

Then she felt something. "Billy! Is that you?"

"Is *what* me?"

"I felt something."

"I don't think it was me," said Billy, though he had no way of supporting his statement.

"Wait a second." It could have been a second. It could have been a hundred years before she said, "I think it's tweed."

"What?"

"Tweed. You know, the fabric."

"Can you see it?"

"No. I can't see anything."

"Then how do you know it's tweed!?"

"Don't yell at me."

Billy realized that he couldn't hear his own voice, but thought he might have been yelling. "Sorry."

"I don't know how I know it's tweed, but it definitely is. It's a tweed jacket."

"Augh!" said Billy. "What's that?"

"What?"

"I got something in my mouth."

"What is it?"

"Fur. I have a fur coat in my face. Suzy! I told you to think about your lab. How did we end up in your closet?"

"I was thinking about my lab, and this isn't my closet."

"How do you know?"

"I don't own any tweed! ... or fur!"

"Okay, you don't have to shout either."

It was Suzy's turn to have the strange sensation of not hearing her own voice. "Billy..." an impossible idea crept into her head. "I don't think we're in a closet."

"It's dark, quiet, and we're surrounded by clothes, where else could we be?"

"A wardrobe," said Suzy. "As in *The Lion, The Witch And...*"

"Suzy! I told you to think about your lab, not your favorite book!"

"How is this my fault?"

"Because I never read *The Lion, The Witch and The Wardrobe*."

"Billy? Seriously?"

"Suzy! I don't think this is the time—"

"I gave you my copy."

"Suzy—"

"You told me you read it."

"I watched the movie, okay?"

"You're impossible."

"And yet I exist none-the... wait a minute, maybe I don't."

"You annoy me, therefore you are," said Suzy, paraphrasing Descartes.

"Will you focus on your lab?"

"I've been thinking about my lab the whole time, but somehow we've landed in an armoire in 1940s rural England."

"That also happens to be imaginary."

"Where's the wand?"

"I don't know. In my hand, I suppose."

"Where's your hand?"

"Should be on the end of my arm, but I have no idea where that is."

"Is your finger still on the button?"

"I don't know."

A flash of red sheet lightning filled the nothingness, and a low roll of thunder prowled around them.

"Suzy?" Billy's question was as much to ask if she was still there as to get her attention.

"Yeah?" There was fear in her voice.

"Don't get scared. It gets bad when you're scared." Billy concentrated as hard as he could on taking his finger off the button.

Janice sat alone in the ruins of her daughter's basement lab, nearly every drop of life drained out of her. When Suzy disappeared from the station there was pandemonium. Every cop in the city went on alert. She couldn't have been gone more than a minute when perimeters sprang up around the building, around the block, around the neighborhood. Janice went through every human emotion on the dark end of the spectrum. After several hours they told her to go home in case Suzy showed up there. They'd call her if they had any news that wasn't already reported on television.

After searching the whole house for any sign of her—even walking down to the Bobble's trailer and talking to an equally distraught Peter—she found herself in Suzy's lab wondering how her sweet baby girl ended up with Bunsen burners as playthings. "Why couldn't you have been into Barbie dolls and boys?" she asked the air.

"Because her father would have none of that silliness," said a man silhouetted in the doorway.

General Henry Quinofski was every bit the hero Janice had fallen in love with so many years ago, and she was as happy to see him now as she was when they first met. She flew into his arms and let loose the tears she hadn't dared shed until now.

"I got here as soon as I could," he whispered. He held her tight while she cried out the stress of the past fourteen hours. She had kept him up-to-date on the events by cell phone until he'd gotten on a plane to come home. That was before Suzy went missing.

"Where is she?" asked Henry.

"She's…gone." She expected her husband to explode over the news. She didn't expect the room to, but it did. A bright flash, a loud crack, and a cold blast of air rocked the couple nearly off their feet.

"Mom? Dad?" said Suzy. "Wow! I'm home!"

"What in the Sam Hill…?" said her father.

"Oh, thank the laws of physics," said Billy when he realized they were both where he hoped they'd be and in one piece. Then he noticed Suzy's dad. "Hi, General, sir." He was still holding Suzy tight, then got nervous and let her go.

"Dad, you're home." She left Billy and dove into her parents' arms.

"Yes, and so are you," he said.

Janice held her only child out at arm's length to get

a look at her. "Are you okay?" Before Suzy could answer, Mrs. Quinofski hugged her again. "Of course you are. You're here. You're fine. I know you're fine."

I'm fine, too, thought Billy.

Mrs. Quinofski took Suzy by the hand. "We have to call the police right away." She dragged her daughter straight to the landline phone. "I promised them I'd call if you turned up."

General Quinofski followed. "Turned up? Was she missing?"

Suzy explained. "Dad, you won't believe it..."

But Billy didn't hear the rest of the conversation, as he'd been fixated on one word—*police.* Suzy was with her family. He was alone and in trouble. Fortunately for him, he had an expert on trouble in his family. As far as Billy was concerned there was only one thing for him to do.

Run!

Twelve

The Fugitive

BILLY HAD NEVER BEEN the athletic type, but had done some running before, mostly in PE. Kickball, running to first base (he never had a chance to run to second). Punishment, running laps. Dodge ball, running away. Prior to that night, he'd have said he ran for his life in dodge ball, but compared to the real thing, escaping a soft red rubber ball was a walk in the park.

Truly running for his life included an infusion of adrenaline that made it more like flying. He kicked into a gear he didn't know he had, as he heard distance sirens getting closer.

The guard gate ahead never meant anything to Billy before, except that it was about the halfway point to home. This time Billy wondered if Suzy's dad would have him stopped. Billy didn't take any chances. He kept running.

"Night, Billy," said the private on duty.
"Night," Billy said over his shoulder.
"Where's the fire?"

Billy started to answer, but then heard the phone ring in the guard's booth. He kept running to the sound of, "Yeah, he just ran past. Want me to go after him?" Two-hundred yards of hard running later, Billy figured the answer to that question had been no.

While the front of his brain was in full panic mode, his background thoughts tried to work out exactly what was happening. His wand worked. He didn't know how, exactly, but it worked. He wanted to disappear and he did. He wanted them to go to Suzy's lab and they did, eventually. Judging by the night sky, those things took some time, no doubt due to the Narnia detour—which he couldn't figure out—and his first journey into complete nothingness.

But he couldn't dwell on that now. Survival was the order of the hour.

He came up on the trailerhood and stopped at the tree line in the woods across from the main road. From there he could see his home. A police car was parked across the street from his trailer, but other than that, no suspicious cars or people could be seen. On the freeway he saw four more cops fly by, lights and sirens blazing, heading south. They'd have to take the Bella street exit and circle back. He had maybe ten minutes, and it was a twelve-minute walk.

More running.

His eyes tried to keep him from twisting an ankle in the ruts and rocks of the field between him and the trailer park, while his head worked on a new thought: his wand.

He could use it to zap himself home. Or could he?

Would that be faster, or would he be stuck in the magical universe until he could manage to find his way out again?

No time to think about that now, the cops were on the exit ramp and heading his way.

Once inside the park, he took the road that paralleled his to avoid the police in front of the house. He came up to the back of the trailer. "Peter," he said under his brother's window. "Peter, wake up, it's me!"

After some rattling of the screen and progressively louder pleas, Peter's light went on.

"Billy?" It sounded like Peter was looking in the hall.

"Peter, I'm out here."

After a second, Peter stuck his face in the window. "Billy, you're alive."

"Yeah, and I'm in trouble, too."

Peter could hear the sirens coming. "Meet you at the car, and keep your head down. They've been watching the house."

Billy blessed the fates for giving him a brother as smart about trouble as Billy was physics. When he crept up to the car, he could hear Peter talking to someone.

"What do you mean, 'what's taking me so long?' honey? It's two o'clock in the morning, I had to wake up."

Billy peeked around to see that Peter was putting on a shirt while talking a little bit too loudly on his cell phone.

"Honey… Honey… I'm on my way, okay?"

He got to the car, and while still holding the phone to his ear, whispered, "Don't open the door. Come in through my side and get in the back."

"Okay," Billy whispered back.

Peter opened the car door, then walked away like he

was losing the phone signal. "Honey? Can you hear me?" he said back into the phone loud enough for the whole neighborhood to hear, "I can't drive while you're on the phone, so the sooner you hang up, the sooner I'll be there. Okay. I love you, too." He pocketed his phone and got in the car.

"You in?" Peter whispered.

"Yeah."

"Get on the floor and cover yourself with the blanket."

The blanket was for what Peter called "emergency picnics" with the girls he dated. It was lousy with grass, pollen, rag weed, and any number of things Billy was allergic to.

"Do you know where we're going, or are we running wild?" asked Peter as he pretended to check his hair in the rearview mirror, but in fact had one eye on the cop walking toward him from across the street.

"No idea," said Billy.

"Quiet, here's the cop."

Peter rolled down his window. "Hey, officer. Any sign of Billy?"

"I was about to ask you the same thing," said the patrolman.

"Officer Carl, is that you?"

"That's me, Peter."

"It's been a long time. How long has it been?"

"Not long enough."

"No, I've been good," said Peter as calm as if he were talking to an old friend, which in a strange way he was. "My parole is done. I'm a working adult now. You got me through some difficult years, Officer Carl, did I ever say thank you?"

"Funny, Peter," he said, shining a flashlight inside the

'67 Dodge. "Where are you heading at this hour?"

Billy saw the light shine through the blanket and was sure he'd been caught.

"Girlfriend trouble," said Peter. "Don't ask me for specifics, because I don't have a clue, but I think Billy's disappearance is freaking her out."

"Or maybe your brother, turned up over at her place?" Obviously, Officer Carl hadn't seen Billy.

"Carl, you didn't even know I had a little brother until this whole thing stirred up."

"Yeah, well, it looks like he's following in the family footsteps. First your father, then you, your mother, now your brother. There hasn't been a Bobble in this town that didn't go bad."

My father, thought Billy. *What did this cop know of my father?*

Peter didn't like the conversation. "That badge doesn't give you the right to talk that way about my family."

"No," said Carl, "but your family's actions do."

Like it or not, Peter had been around enough to know when he was being baited. "Tell you what, Carl, I'm going to drive away now. Are you going to follow me, or are you going to watch the house?"

"Oh, I'm following you."

"Well," said Peter, "You'd best hurry then." He revved the super-charged engine of his old-school muscle car and Carl bolted for his black & white.

Peter laughed and pulled away nice, slow and legal.

"Why aren't you driving faster?" Billy asked from under the blanket. He could remember times when Peter had scared the crap out of him in that car with high speed antics. If there was a time for fancy driving, Billy figured it was now.

"First rule of being a fugitive, kid: you can't out run a radio." As they took a left onto the main road, four patrol cars with lights and sirens blaring turned into the complex, and Billy thought, *my wand can out run a radio, easy.*

The rules to everything would change, thanks to Billy Bobble.

"So your wand worked, huh?" Peter asked his empty backseat. He'd gotten on to the road toward town. Carl was clearly behind him and seemed content to follow at a distance. They had a little time to talk.

"Sort of, yeah, I guess. Can I get up now?"

"No, he'll see you for sure."

Billy sneezed.

"Hey, cut that out. You never know when he'll pull up at a stoplight or something."

"Sorry, I have allergies, you know."

"So? Zap them away with your magic."

"I don't know how. Can we please get someplace where I can breathe?"

"I'm working on that." Peter had spent much of his youth dodging authority, but this was a tight spot. He started thinking out loud. "He checked out the car when we left home, so he's confident you're not with me. That means he's expecting me to come to you."

Billy sneezed again.

"Bless you."

"Thank you."

"Stop sneezing."

"I'm trying."

Peter went back to figuring. "He knew there was backup on the way to the house, so he's no doubt told them he was leaving to follow me. He's not going to take his eyes off me. I need him to take his eyes off the car, so you…" He thought for a second then, "got it!"

By comparison, a patrol officer's uniform has got nothing on a four star general's. Quinofski knew this when he put on his jacket, straightened his tie, and told his daughter to stay put in her bedroom before answering the pounding at his door.

In the short time it took the black & white to get to them, Janice had briefed Henry on the situation, mostly Suzy's escape from the station. When Suzy told him how they'd used the wand, her father didn't say a thing, but Suzy noticed a change in his demeanor. "Dad, you've got your General's Face on."

That's when the cops showed up. Suzy did as she was told. She went to her room, but that didn't mean she couldn't peek out to see what transpired.

Her father opened the door to find a young cop shaking in his boots. "You're out of your league, son." The patrolman stood on the porch surrounded by Military Police and more blue and red flashing lights than Suzy had ever seen. Her father remained cool. "This is *my* world. You have no jurisdiction here."

"We, uh…"

"In my world, the heavily armed MPs who surround you are the law, and they take orders from me."

Suzy thought the poor young officer might very well have wet himself had Detective Danner not come to his rescue. "Is that a threat, General?" he said from the back of the crowd of people massed at the house.

"Just stating a fact, Detective." Quinofski's tone matched Danner's, calm and professional.

"We're in pursuit of an escapee, who also happens to be your daughter."

"It takes all these men to arrest one 12-year-old?"

"We're also concerned for her safety."

"I have spoken with my daughter," said the General, "and I assure you she is in good health and good hands."

"So you know her whereabouts, then?"

In these modern times a man or woman does not rise to the rank and responsibility of a four-star general without recognizing the subtlest of legalese. If he admitted to knowing where she was, he could be arrested for obstruction of justice then and there. "Detective," said Quinofski, "It's late. I'm sure both of us would rather be sleeping right now, so unless you want to wake up the Supreme Court to authorize a civilian search warrant on a military base, I suggest you go home and we can all settle this thing in the morning."

Danner looked past the General to Mrs. Quinofski.

"It's fine," she said, answering his unasked question.

Then to Suzy's horror, Danner peered down the hall and locked eyes with her. She should have snatched her head back behind her door, but she was too frightened to move, so she smiled. When Danner didn't come charging inside with guns blazing, she went so far as to wave.

Danner then said to her Dad, "Glad to know she's okay. Everything else is... well. Eight o'clock, my office."

"You're a wise man, Detective."

"We're still on the lookout for the Bobble kid."

"We've seen him," said Quinofski. "He's alive and scared. He ran out of here, probably back to his house."

"Okay, so I don't have two dead kids on my hands. Good. Thank you for that information, and I'll see you in the morning, sir."

With that, both men went their separate ways.

"Take this."

Peter slipped a wad of money wrapped around a business card under the back cushion of the front seat. "Thanks." Billy saw that the card was from a motel.

"If all else fails, go to that motel. Sleeping in a toilet might be more sanitary, but the night clerk never asks questions about who comes and goes—and he never sees anything."

The plan was simple, but that didn't make it any less scary.

The trick was to do it in such a manner as to not get Peter in any trouble. With his juvenile record, one wrong step and they'd lock him up for sure. With their mother on shaky mental health ground, if Peter couldn't take care of him, Billy might land in foster care once the authorities found him.

"Try my friend's house first, okay?"

"Okay."

"You remember the directions?"

"Yeah." Billy sneezed.

"Quiet. Carl's pulling up."

Billy checked the blanket to make sure he was well covered, then held his nose.

Peter whispered, "Good luck," and got out of the car.

Billy heard a car pull up and a window roll down. Then Peter said, "I'm going to buy my girlfriend some flowers and ice cream in the grocery story, so you sit tight, Officer Carl, I'll be right back." Billy heard the car engine turn off.

The idea was that cops always thought Peter was up to something, so they'd never do what he told them. That made them easy to manipulate.

"Don't sneeze or anything, 'cause you might miss something." That last bit had been for Billy's sake. Carl must have been within easy earshot. Billy squeezed his nose tighter, and listened with all of his might.

Ten minutes past. Tears streamed down his face as his allergies begged to expel whatever was bothering them. It was about then that he wondered why he couldn't just turn himself in. In the grand scheme of things he hadn't really done anything wrong. Well, breaking Suzy out of jail was probably a crime, but—

What was that?

He listened hard.

Nothing.

Eventually, Carl would realize that Peter wasn't coming back, at which point he'd go after him. That would leave the car unwatched long enough for Billy to escape out back and cut through to the neighborhood two blocks away. Carl would find Peter wrestling with the choice of which flowers to buy, doing nothing wrong, while Billy went to Peter's friend's house looking for a place to crash.

Billy heard a car door open right next to him and his blood went cold. Was someone getting into the car with him? Was it Peter? Should he say something?

"No," was apparently the answer to all of those questions. Billy could hear footsteps crunch on the asphalt, then he saw a flashlight shine over him one more time. Billy's urge to sneeze was overpowering, but if he so much as breathed heavily, Carl was sure to notice.

The light lingered over the blanket for a long time before it clicked off. Billy heard the steps walk away. When they faded completely, he executed his part of the plan. Quietly, he opened the passenger door, crawled out, quietly closed it, and ran to the back of the parking lot. There he found a fence that animals must have burrowed under to get to the dumpster right next to it. Billy got down in the dirt and garbage to squeeze himself through to the other side. From there, he peeked through a tiny hole in the fence. Officer Carl was nowhere in sight, so Billy indulged himself. He let out a sneeze that might have registered on the Richter scale.

"Bless you!"

Billy jumped three feet in the air. He had no idea anyone was behind him.

"I thought that cop would never leave."

Once Billy swallowed his heart out of his throat, he saw that his chatty companion was a crazy old homeless guy. He was like every other soiled sad sack who might push a grocery cart full of recyclables or beg change outside of a liquor store—except he wore laurels on his head like some kind of ancient Greek VIP.

"And if he didn't leave," said the man, as he handed Billy a clean tissue, "you and I wouldn't get to have our little talk, would we... Billy Bobble?"

Thirteen

Prometheus Returns

"How do you know my name?"

Billy was used to having more answers than questions in his life, but he was smart enough to know that the dumbest question is the one unasked.

"I know a lot of things," said the man, "like the fact that we shouldn't talk here."

"I don't think we should talk at all." Billy walked away, came back, took the tissue, then walked away again.

The bum didn't move. "Your friend's parents may call the police."

"How do you know?"

"I don't."

"You're starting to freak me out, old weird guy." Billy ran for all he was worth toward Peter's friend's house.

The house was nicer than Billy's trailer home, but not by a lot. The neighborhood might have once been middle class, but that was a long time ago. *Millstone Concrete Co. 1950* was stamped into the wavy, rooted, sidewalk. Billy wouldn't have noticed, but he was told to look for some stairs leading down from the sidewalk around to the back of one of the brick houses.

He found the stairs and followed them to a basement entrance with an old aluminum glass-and-screen door in front of a wooden, window-paned one. Billy expected a bright security light to go off when he walked up, but instead, only candlelight flickered through sheer pastel curtains that Billy thought didn't match the rest of the house.

As Peter told him to do, he tapped lightly on the door. "Hello," he said in a stage whisper. "Peter sent me."

A choking cloud of incense and perfumes wafted around Billy as the door flung open, revealing Linda Lubinski, a vision in gothic black chic. "You're kidding me!"

"Linda?" Billy was as shocked as she was.

"Your brother has got some nerve."

"I—"

"He thinks I'm going to let *you* stay here?"

"But—"

"You're the most wanted kid in the state."

That excuse was better than some Billy might have thought she'd come up with—like, I hate you, or...

"Never mind that you tried to *kill me*!"

...That one. Billy had to put a stop to the wild fire before it could spread. "I didn't. I didn't think—"

"Neither did your bother," she said. "Good night."

She tried to slam the door, but Billy managed to pitifully wedge himself in the way. "I just need a place to sleep."

"The only reason I'm not calling the cops right now is because of Peter."

Thoughts swarmed Billy's head, *Why would she...? What did she and Peter...?* but all he managed to say was, "What?"

But his stammering question would have to wait for an answer, as Linda's father called from upstairs. "Linda?"

She ignored him, except to tell Billy, "I can't promise my parents have the same loyalty I have to your brother."

A light switched on upstairs. "Linda, are you okay?"

Billy didn't know what to do, so Linda told him. "Run, little boy," she whispered. "Run!"

Billy didn't know this neighborhood well, but he recognized a grove of trees when he saw one. He dove into the woods to catch his breath out of sight and take a closer look at the motel business card. It was ratty and old. It must have been in Peter's car for years. Before Peter had said "If all else fails" and slipped him the money, he mentioned some other friends to go to, so Billy put the card back in his pocket.

Other friends, he thought. *Other friends like Linda?* How well did Peter know Linda? Did he know she was a witch?

"Yes," said the man, who ambled toward Billy from the woods. It was the same homeless guy from earlier. "The two hundred twenty-five dollars and seventeen cents you have is enough for the motel."

Billy stopped. Peter had slipped him a stack of twenties under the seat. It could have been two-hundred and twenty dollars. Billy had five on him before that, but… "I don't have seventeen cents."

"Check your back pocket." The stranger was beginning to look a little less rough around the edges, and Billy couldn't shake the feeling that he was somehow familiar.

He pulled a dime, nickel, two pennies, and a forgotten pack of gum from his back pocket. "What are you, some kind of magician?"

"I'm not the one with a magic wand, Mr. Bobble."

"Okay," said Billy, trying not to be as scared as he actually was. "You know my name. You know how much money I have, and seem to know what I'm thinking. Shouldn't I know something about you?"

"Hmmmm… no," said the man. "Not yet. Let's get you settled first." With that, he took the lead, walking toward the neighborhood.

Billy noticed that his ragged patchwork of clothes formed a cape that dragged the ground behind him. He wasn't exactly sure why, but he followed. "If I can't know who you are, can I at least know what to call you?"

"One of your predecessors called me Prometheus."

"The Greek god who gave fire to man?"

"Not a god, actually, he was a Titan."

"'He was,'" noted Billy, "meaning, you aren't?"

"Do you believe in the Greek Pantheon?"

"Up until now I hadn't given it much thought."

"You're going to have to give thought to a lot of things you hadn't before, Billy."

"Yeah, like running from the cops and talking to crazy homeless guys."

"Billy." Prometheus, for lack of a better name, stopped. "You've changed your world forever. E = mc² is no longer the most powerful force in the universe. Your wand is."

Billy looked at the stick in his hand and wished he could figure out how it really worked.

There was a big party in the neighborhood. From three blocks away Billy could hear a dozen familiar voices. Many of them talking about the explosion at school and wondering aloud where Billy was. He decided it was best to skip all of the friends and go to plan C.

Billy and his old companion circled back to the main strip where Peter had parked. He and officer Carl were gone. The motel was a half-block down the street.

"I'll be fine from here," Billy told the stranger.

"Don't you trust me, Billy Bobble?"

"No, I don't. I don't even know you."

"Good boy. Trust, but don't be stupid," he said. "An equal amount of trust and suspicion is given to everyone, the rest must be earned."

Blah, blah, blah. Billy walked into the office, expecting the old guy would follow, but when he turned around no one was there.

"You're letting the air-conditioning out," said the desk clerk without looking up from his laptop computer.

"What?"

"Close the door."

"Oh. Sorry." Billy closed the door and walked up to the desk, where he stood politely, not wanting to interrupt the man from his business on the computer.

"You waiting on a bus?"

"What?"

The man still didn't look up from his computer, and from the growth of whiskers on his face, Billy thought he might not have moved from that spot in days. "What do you want?"

"Oh. I'd like a room, please."

"Twenty bucks for an hour. Fifty for the whole night."

"That's crazy. Who would ever book a hotel room for just an hour?"

The man finally took his eyes off the computer to stare at Billy like he was from another planet. After enough time had passed to make Billy uncomfortable, the man spoke up. "So, you want the whole night, then?"

"Yes, sir."

"Fifty bucks."

Billy put three twenties on the counter. The man replaced the money with a key. "Back outside to the right."

"Uh... I gave you sixty dollars."

"Yeah? What are you going to do, complain?"

Billy had tucked his wand up the sleeve of his shirt and for a moment he thought about what he might do with it. In the end, he did nothing. Not because he didn't want to, or because he didn't know how, but because nothing was the right thing to do. Yeah, the guy was a jerk, possibly even a criminal, but it was those qualities that allowed a kid his age to check into a room with no ID and no questions. Ten dollars was a cheap tip in those circumstances.

"No," said Billy as he left. "Dinner's on me."

"This is a good place for our talk."

The old man startled Billy so badly outside his room that he dropped his key. Mr. Prometheus picked it up but didn't give it back, and didn't open the door.

Billy noticed he had changed his look. He was still older than the earth, but was now clean, with long white hair and a beard to match. What had been a robe made of rags was now a black billowing garment with gold designs of stars and moons. In this guise, Billy thought he could pass for Merlin, Gandalf, Dumbledore, or any of the iconic Wizards of the Sceptered Isle if he weren't walking around the parking lot of a cheap motel.

"You changed your form," said Billy.

"What?" He checked out his appearance in the reflection of a hotel room window. "Oh, yes. Occupational necessity. Why do you think that is?"

"I don't know," Billy said, the typical reflex answer of a 12-year-old with a tired brain.

"Oh, but you do. You definitely know," said the wizard. "So the question becomes, 'why do you NOT think of why I change form?'"

"No," said Billy, "The question is still, 'Who are you?'"

"That's a complicated question."

"I'm used to complicated answers. I can handle it."

"You know," said the old man. He stopped to stroke his beard, which gave Billy the impression he was thinking back… and back… and back… and back to nearly the dawn of time, "Of all the humans I've dealt with, I think you're the first to ask me that question who might actually listen to, and understand, the answer."

"Goodie for me."

"I am a being of the Quantum World," he said. "As much as you might think you know about existence, without a deep understanding of my world, you can only know half the story."

"I know all about quantum physics."

"Physics, sure. Great. I know all about the physics of your world, too, but it doesn't mean I can pick out the right thing to wear to a June wedding in Tucson. Does knowing physics make you more popular? Does it help you understand social or political situations? Does brilliance in physics help you get the girl?"

"I think I'm too young for girls."

"There is more to intellect than what is taught by teachers or measured in tests, just as there is more to the Quantum World than physics."

"Like what?"

"Like consciousness," said the old man. "In your world there are four chemicals that make up life."

"Adenine, guanine, cytosine, thymine," said Billy by rote, thanks to Suzy.

"Mix those up in a test tube any way you like, zap them with any kind of energy, but without consciousness, they will not become life."

"And consciousness comes from the Quantum World?"

"Every amoeba, every plant, every animal, every cell in your body is connected to the Quantum World."

"And my wand breaks that connection?"

"No. Death breaks that connection. Your wand opens a pathway between your physical world and mine. In your world, reality is defined by what you do; in mine, by what you think."

The mysteries of his adventures in magic were becoming a bit more clear. "And if you think that pathway might be like the wardrobe between Earth and Narnia?"

"Then that is where you'll find yourself."

Billy brought the subject back around to what got them stared. "So your physical appearance…?"

"Is defined by the viewer. You see me as a wizard. Others, a god."

"Or a Titan? You've been seen before?"

The wizard gave a wry smile. "There are many ways into my world, Billy. Though, happily, you're one of the first humans I've ever had a decent conversation with."

"Really?" said Billy. Something about that made him proud.

"Most of the others either egomaniacally proclaimed themselves to be prophets, or became so full of self-doubt that they went completely insane."

Billy thought of his mother. "What if they were insane to begin with?"

The old wizard sighed. "One of the many things we share between your world and mine, Billy, is a dependence on Nature. She is… by necessity… extraordinarily, beautifully, and horribly imperfect. So when a life form is not firmly anchored in your world—or begins to lose hold in mine—it can become very hard on them."

Billy weighed the novelty toy in his hand. "Do you think I could push the button on my wand and fix that?"

"I don't know," said the wizard. "It's as new to me as it is to you. But –" he perked up, "I'm glad to hear you ask that question, young Mr. Bobble."

"Yeah? Why's that?"

"Consciousness: Good and Evil. Right and Wrong. Heroes and Villains. Gods and Devils. They are all products of the Quantum World, but manifest themselves in yours. Evil—which often disguises itself as Good—takes advantage of weak minds." He then added as an aside, "It's very important, by the way, that you not confuse intelligence with mental strength. An intelligent but selfish man would have invented your wand and never thought about helping his schizophrenic mother."

"I think I understand," said Billy.

"You'd better," said the wizard, "because the forces of darkness will be after your wand, and they will stop at nothing to get it. They will try to get inside your head. They will use others in your world they already control to manipulate you, to torture you, to bend your will into doing their bidding."

His ominous tone scared Billy as much as his words.

"From now on, young man, you are not paranoid. They *are* watching you. They *are* out to get you. For you have a great power, and with great power must come great responsibility."

Billy heard and understood everything being told to

him, but the familiarity of that last bit threw him a curve. "Isn't that from the Bible?"

"I'm not sure," said the wizard. "I got it from Stan Lee. *Amazing Fantasy #15.*"

"You mean *Spiderman*?!"

"Does that make it any less true?"

"No. In fact, it makes it more clear."

"Good."

It was clear. At 12 years old Billy held his life's work in his hand. From this point forward, everything he was would revolve around his wand, his great power, his great responsibility.

"The question that will haunt you in your sleep…" said the wizened wizard with a pause that sent a chill down Billy's spine. This day could already fuel a lifetime of nightmares, what could be so bad as to earn a special warning? "…is exactly how I am holding onto this key." He handed it to Billy as he said it, then, "My work here is done."

Just that quickly, Billy was alone in the parking lot.

"Hello!"

Nothing.

"Hey, old guy."

Nothing.

"Where did you go?"

Still nothing, so Billy went to his room, texted Peter to say where he was, collapsed on the bed, and to his great surprise, was asleep in an instant.

Fourteen

The Quantum Cats

"**D**o you know the whereabouts of Billy Bobble?"

"No."

General Quinofski's answer to Detective Danner's question was honest. He did not know exactly where Billy was, but from a phone conversation with Peter that morning, he knew Billy was safe and that Peter would keep an eye on him until this meeting was over.

"Suzy?" asked Danner.

"All I know is that he's alive and well," she said, "so we should be able to go home."

"I don't know about that," said Danner.

"Detective," said Janice, "you were questioning Suzy about Billy's disappearance. Well, he's back so you have no reason to hold her."

"About that," said Danner to Suzy, "you said Billy appeared in the room with you. How exactly did he do that?"

"I told you, the same way he disappeared."

"You told me –"

"You've got to have a security video," Suzy interrupted. "Look for yourself."

General Quinofski read a text he'd just received on his cell phone. It was the trump card he'd been waiting for. "Actually, you no longer have access to any security footage." To Danner's what-are-you-talking-about reaction, he said, "All matters concerning the children's invention have been classified Top Secret by the President of the United States, including this conversation."

"You can't do that," said Danner.

He held up his phone. "I already have."

"But—"

"Detective, we can, and probably will, fight this out in the courts, but consider my point of view: A 12-year-old boy entered a secure facility, which for him was behind enemy lines, extracted a prisoner, and returned her safely to base camp. It would take me two weeks with a special ops unit to pull that off, and I'm not sure they could do it at all."

Danner smirked in a way that suggested he thought that was a compliment to the police force.

"I don't know what these kids are playing at," said the General, "but I don't want anyone else to know, either. From now on, this is a military operation. You and your staff are to forget it happened, you understand?"

"How are we supposed to do that?" asked Danner, still not sure he'd accept this action.

"Easy. Keep thinking of the sentence for treason."

Prrrrrrr … meow … Prrrrrrrrr

Billy was awakened by a friendly black cat impatient to be fed. "Good morning, kitty." He took comfort in petting the cat before questioning how it got into his room, who it might belong to, or where he was. For a brief moment he just wanted to enjoy the simplicity of a purring cat.

But the animal had better ideas. She jumped off the bed, into a chair across the room, and transformed into a little old lady. At least, Billy thought there was a lady under her bundle of clothes. She wore several scarves of assorted colors, a man's felt hat, a rough overcoat, and black rubber boots on her feet.

"Please tell me I'm dreaming."

"Oh, dear," said the tiny woman as she unraveled scarf after scarf from her gray head. "You're going to have a hard time telling the difference between dreams and realities from now on, Billy, since for you, there isn't much of one." Her voice was like an un-oiled gate, but still had a purr to it.

"So…" Billy started. He wanted to avoid the obvious who-are-you question and see if he couldn't answer it himself. "…if last night I talked with a Prometheus-Wizard, would that make you a Pandora-Witch?"

"If you wish."

"If *I* wish," said Billy. He quickly realized, "You're the same person I talked to last night."

The woman gave Billy's guess a nod of respect. "I'm

not sure 'person' is the right word, but no, I am a different consciousness. Of course, I'm not the important one here, young Billy. I'm not the one with the magic wand."

"I'm starting to think I should break that thing and forget it ever existed."

"Pandora said the same thing about her box."

Billy took the point. The troubles Pandora released could never be recaptured any more than Einstein could have erased E=mc² or all the king's horses and men could have put Humpty Dumpty back together again. Then he thought of what he learned last night. He is not paranoid. They really are out to get him, so: "Who you are *is* important. How do I know you're not evil?"

The woman laughed, or purred, it was hard to tell the difference, and said, "Search your heart, young one."

Billy had to scramble to get his wits about him. This innocent-looking old lady was a quantum being. She might be after his wand. If he was going to get the upper hand he'd have to recall everything he knew about such creatures, which was limited to the conversation he'd had last night. He concentrated on a different façade for the consciousness that sat before him. As he did, the ancient, brittle, woman transformed into a girl about his age dressed kind of like… Huckleberry Finn.

"I was trying to imagine you into a guy-friend," he told the shade.

"You'll find there are limits to how you can change one of us," she said. "For example, consciousness is gender-specific. Whatever form I take, I'll always be female."

"Good to know," said Billy. "At least you're closer to my age. Now who are you?"

"The Teacher sent me."

"The who?"

"The Teacher. You talked with him last night."

"You mean the old guy, looks like Merlin?"

"Actually, he was Merlin, but that's another story."

"So, *Merlin* sent you." A good part of Billy couldn't believe he was having this conversation. "Does that mean you're Excalibur or something."

"Don't be stupid. Excalibur was in inanimate object. I'm more like… the Lady of the Lake. I'm a consciousness. I'm your familiar."

"My what?"

The girl sighed. "You know, for a boy who invented a magic wand, you don't know much about witches and wizards."

"I don't know anything about witches and wizards. What's a familiar?"

"Every witch has their helper-animal, like a black cat or something."

"Oh, right, right!" Billy's a-ha moment was so strong that his familiar changed into a large, white, snow owl.

"Argh! J.K. Rowling!" said the owl—though, Billy wasn't sure if she said it, or he heard it in his head. Either way, the owl shook itself out and became the Huck Finn girl again, only dressed more appropriately for a current day Tomboy.

"So what does a familiar do?"

"Anything you want done," said the girl.

"Anything at all?"

"There are limits," she warned.

"Like what?"

"Like, I'm mostly a figment of your imagination, but I'm also part of the collective consciousness, so others can see me, but… it's like… your connection to the Quantum World is what brought me here, but other people's acceptance of my existence is what makes me real to them. Does that make sense?"

"Not a bit."

"Okay, well, just don't ask a group of people to describe me, because it's likely to be different for everyone. That's why we usually take on animal forms. To humans, all black cats look alike."

"So no fashion shows. What else?"

"Lots of things. I'll let you know when they come up."

"Okay. Cool…" said Billy. He wasn't sure what to do with a consciousness that would do anything he wanted done. He decided not to think about that for the moment. "What's your name?"

"Whatever you want it to be."

"No, really, I don't care what it is. I just want to know."

"So do I," she said. "I don't have a name until you give me one."

Billy didn't like this at all. He and Peter had a pet cat for a while. They called it "cat." Billy used to joke that he didn't speak cat, so he didn't know it's real name. In fact, he just couldn't come up with one. "What would you like your name to be," he asked, since obviously they did speak the same language.

"In our world, we don't have names."

"How is that possible?"

"Think about your brother," she said. Billy did. "Are you thinking of his name, or everything about him all at once?"

"I thought how he used to be a jerk, but recently he's been okay. I thought… I don't know, all kinds of stuff."

"Right. That's who your brother is. 'Peter' is just a label."

"How do you know about my brother?"

"I know what you know."

"Oh, sure. You know what I know, but you don't know what you want to be called."

"No preference whatsoever."

"Great." Billy thought for a second, then: "Okay, how about this. You're my familiar, so I'll call you … 'fam.' Wait. No. Fame. How about that? Fame."

"Fame it is. Pleased to meet you," she said, offering her hand to shake.

Billy took it. "The pleasure's mine, Fame." Her hand had the odd sensation of not actually being there, like matter without mass.

"What can I do for you?" she asked, which knocked the observation out of Billy's head.

She would do pretty much whatever he asked her to. With great power comes great responsibility, with this little bit of power comes a lot of little decisions. Then he thought of something. "Could you tell me how my wand works?"

"You should know that. You built it."

"I know that it breaks the connection between Time and Space."

"And that puts you in the Quantum World."

"Yeah… I guess." Billy got an odd feeling in the pit of his stomach. The more he tried to figure out his wand, the less he could grasp it, and the worse the feeling got. He wondered if this is what other kids went through in school every day. No wonder why they hated it.

"The explosion of a super nova can go completely unnoticed in the Quantum World," said Fame, "but one little boy's nightmare can rip it apart."

"I don't understand."

"Energy is matter; matter is energy," said Fame. "An explosion changes one into the other. So what? A thought gives them life, and your wand makes them real."

"Billy!" It was Peter calling out to him from the parking lot.

Billy looked out of the window to see his mother, Peter, Suzy, her dad, and what appeared to be two police detectives in the parking lot.

"Come on out, Billy," said Suzy. "All has been forgiven."

On hearing her, Fame waved at Billy and disappeared with a Cheshire smile.

Fifteen

If I Had a Hammer & Other Familiar Songs

"So, the wand's effect is limited to the source DNA inside it?"

General Quinofski insisted on a thorough debriefing of every detail of the creation of the wand. He, Billy and Suzy had been holed up in the basement lab all morning. Suzy kept her mouth shut. She figured she'd told the story yesterday and her dad had confiscated the video so he could watch it anytime he wanted. She listened as Billy finished his version of the story without interruption, but now was her time to speak up. "No Dad, not completely. I transported with Billy from the police station to here."

"Via the wardrobe," said Billy, "which you thought of."

"I did not! The wand obviously picked up on your guilt for having not read the book."

The General ignored their spat with such intensity that it ended.

He brewed in silence for a minute, while Billy thought of what he hadn't revealed. He told them about the Teacher, but not about Fame. He wasn't sure why. For some reason, an old weird guy behind a dumpster seemed okay to talk about, but Fame didn't. He wasn't sure how Suzy would feel about him having a personal servant. Especially one who was a girl. Then he wasn't sure why her being a girl should have made any difference to either one of them. Must have been another gut feeling, or maybe he felt guilty because Suzy did as much work on the wand as Billy did. Why shouldn't she have a familiar, too?

General Quinofski jotted down some notes on a pad. "Billy, I know you don't have a lot of reason to trust me, but—"

"Of course I do, sir," said Billy. Aside from his brother, Suzy's Dad was the only adult man Billy really knew. He had male teachers, of course, and Professor Menaus at Oakridge, but he didn't know them very well.

"Good," said the General, "because what you have achieved is... a game-changer. I promise I will never take that away from either of you."

"But...?" asked Suzy, who knew there had to be more to this.

"But," said her father, "we need to be careful. The world doesn't like to have the game changed too quickly. Can you imagine if everyone had one of these teleportation sticks? How would we stop bank robbers, or protect the President? No one would need cars anymore, so what would happen to the economy when all those who used to build them are suddenly out of work?"

"It's more than teleportation," said Billy. "It turns thoughts into reality."

"All the more reason to keep it a secret, at least for now," said the General. He drifted off for a moment before he changed the subject. "Have you had breakfast yet, Billy?"

"No sir, not yet."

"You must be hungry."

"Now that you mention it, yeah. I'm starving."

"So, if you thought about whipping us up a big brunch buffet and then activated your wand…?"

"I don't know what would happen."

"Want to give it a shot?"

Billy looked to Suzy. "What?" she said. "It's not like we'll get in any more trouble. Dad's the responsible one now."

"Sure," said Billy, "why not? I've got a magic wand, it's about time I started enjoying it."

They cleared the basement of everything but the wooden lab table. Janice worried herself silly upstairs, until she realized standing above a possible explosion in the basement might not be a good idea, so she waited outside. General Quinofski set up a video camera. They all donned safety goggles, and Billy went to work.

"One big brunch buffet coming up," he said before he pushed the button on his wand.

Wham! They got a brunch buffet all right. The trouble was, the cold explosion blew the food, plates, utensils, and everything else all over the walls. Nearly every inch of the basement and all its inhabitants were covered in food.

"Oh, man!" Billy rushed over to help the General to his feet. "I'm sorry, sir."

"That's okay, Billy, I'm fine."

"Suzy?"

Suzy lay flat on her back in a sea of orange juice, scrambled eggs, hash browns and ketchup. "I'm getting used to it." She looked down at her feet. "The cat's a new addition, though."

Sure enough, Fame, in her black feline form, was licking pancake syrup off Suzy's toes.

"Oh, that's Fame," said Billy, "my, uh…"

You didn't tell them about me? asked Fame.

At the same time, Suzy finished Billy's sentence. "Cat?"

"No," said Billy to Fame, then to Suzy, "I mean, yes."

"You don't have a cat."

"I picked her up at the motel."

"You picked up a strange … never mind," said Suzy, "could you just clean us up?"

"Yes, Billy," said her father. "You've proven you can make matter appear from nothing. Let's see if you can turn it back into nothing."

Billy tapped the stick against his palm. "How do I do this?"

"You're asking us?" said Suzy. "You might as well ask the cat."

I thought you were asking me, Billy heard Fame say. *We don't have wands in the Quantum World, but I'd guess that you have to focus your thoughts more clearly. Your kind use words to represent thoughts, so find the right word.*

"Okay," Billy said to his cat, who to Suzy and the General appeared to just be sitting there attentively.

If you can focus on one word that encapsulates everything about what you want to achieve, I think you'll have better luck.

"One word," said Billy to the cat.

"Yuck, would be my choice," said Suzy.

Yes, said Fame. *Oh, and you should know, I'm not actually talking. You're hearing me in your head.*

"So… they can't hear…" said Billy as he began to realize how crazy he must sound.

"We can hear fine, Billy."

"No, the cat," he said.

"Meow," she said.

"I hear the cat, too," said Suzy.

"Very funny," said Billy to Fame.

No, what's funny is you three, Fame said inside Billy's head. *You should look in a mirror.*

"Billy, when you're ready," said the General.

"Yes sir. I just have to think of the right word…"

"Seriously?" asked Suzy. "You have to think of a magic word?"

"Uh… you could call it that."

All kidding aside, Billy, said the voice in his head, *I recommend the word… 'oops.'*

"That's perfect," said Billy. It captured the thoughts and feelings of the moment and conjured in his head the deepest desire to see the basement back the way it was before this experiment began.

"You're not making any sense, Billy."

Think of the word. Say the word. Push the button, thought Fame.

Billy walked over to the same spot he was in before—in

front of the camera. Suzy and her dad braced for impact. Billy raised his wand, said "Oops!" and pushed the button.

The cold white explosion ripped through the basement as it had before, only this time, instead of blasting stuff all over the place, it reset everything to the way it was before they'd tried to create brunch. All the furniture was back the way it had been. Every speck of mess was gone. Billy looked over at a spanking clean Suzy and her father and beamed with pride.

They, on the other hand, looked past Billy in amazement.

"What?" Billy asked.

"Look behind you, son."

He did. A breakfast buffet worthy of a five star hotel, and Suzy's old lab equipment—good as new, lay before him. Billy picked up a silver spoon and uncovered a matching serving dish. Corned beef hash, his favorite. He scooped it up and took a bite.

"Delicious."

There's trouble.

They had finished their brunch without any more discussion of wands and magic, per the General's orders. Suzy's mom had come running in right after "oops," when all the furniture in the yard disappeared. She found it in place in the basement, and so joined in the brunch feast.

Everyone feared the food at first. The parents remembered a time when people were afraid of eating something cooked in a microwave oven, and there they were about to eat a meal that appeared out of thin air.

It's fine, said Fame to the inside of Billy's mind. *Nothing to worry about.*

Once Billy started eating in earnest, the rest joined in.

It was about that time that the General got a call, which he took outside. Fame had a bad feeling about that, and told Billy there was trouble.

Billy concentrated at the cat. *Can you hear my thoughts, or do I have to talk out loud?*

I hear you loud and clear, said Fame.

Good. What kind of trouble?

I don't know for sure, but that call trumped a magic wand. When Billy didn't respond, she asked, *Would you like me to eavesdrop? It's something we familiars are best at.*

Billy contemplated the moral implications of listening in on an adult's private conversation, and the legal issues of listening in on top secret ones. Then he remembered, "from this point forward, you are not paranoid. They really are after you."

Sure, he thought toward the cat.

Fame ran outside like any ordinary house cat would.

"So…" said Suzy into the awkward silence that filled her father's departure. "How do you propose we do the dishes?"

"The old-fashioned way," said her mom.

"Yeah," said Suzy, "you want to just keep the silver set?"

Janice looked it over. "It is nice. And expensive. What should we do with it?"

"Billy could make it disappear," said Suzy.

Her mother was quick to nix that idea. "No. I've had my fill of explosions for one day."

Just then, Fame came back to report, *A group of special operations soldiers in Pakistan have been captured by terrorists.*

"What?!" said Billy.

"You heard me," said Mrs. Quinofski. "Hank may run the Army, but I run this house. I am putting my foot down. No more magic in the basement. We'll figure out what to do with the silver later."

You really need to get used to the fact that you're the only one who can hear me, said Fame.

"Sorry," said Billy.

"Nothing to be sorry about, Billy, dear. You were doing what you were told."

Yeah, this is going to take practice, thought Billy. He then got back on topic. *Special ops forces captured? What else?*

You're about to find out, said Fame. She scooted out of the way as the General came back inside.

Billy could barely contain himself with the urgency of the situation, but he noticed that General Quinofski acted as if the call had been from the garage about his car or something normal like that.

"Kids, I'll get right to the point." But he didn't. Instead, he got himself another cup of coffee from the urn Billy had concocted. Some cream, too much sugar, a stir, a taste, *then* he got right to the point. "I could make good use of a few of those wands."

Billy had been expecting this all day. In fact, he'd been fantasizing about it for as long as he could remember. Every practical scientist does, or has since Nobel invented dynamite or Einstein unlocked energy from matter. What do you do if your invention might lead to something horrible?

"It's not a weapon," said Billy.

"I appreciate that—" said the General, but Billy cut him short.

"—but then again, neither is a hammer."

"True. A hammer is a tool." To his credit, the General did not rush the boy. At 12 years old Billy had all the pressure of bomb-builder, Robert Oppenheimer, thrust upon him. For the sake of everyone's sanity, this decision should be well thought out.

"If somebody takes my hammer," said Billy, "and bashes somebody else in the head with it, am I responsible for having had the hammer?"

"That would depend, I think," said the General, which surprised Billy. He was expecting a "not at all, so let me take your wand." But instead, "If you'd taken the hammer into a mental hospital in a ward full of people with anger issues, I'd say you did bear some responsibility."

Suzy chimed in. "Yeah, but what if you handed it to a cop who used it to stop a murderer?"

No one said anything for a good long while. Eventually, Billy turned to his cat.

Don't look at me, said Fame. *This technology is as new to us as it is you.*

"Technology," said Billy. "When it comes right down to it, this is a scientific breakthrough like any other. Scientists always say they sit on top of a pyramid of knowledge. And no one is on top for long."

"In the military," said General, "we have a saying, 'Technology never retreats.'"

Billy got to thinking about what the Teacher had told him about Greek mythology, which he knew little about. Most of his knowledge in that area came from reruns of *Xena: Warrior Princess,* but one story did stick from grade school. "Pandora's box can't be closed," he said.

Mrs. Quinofski, who had been silent for most of the conversation, finally spoke up. "Do you know what else was in Pandora's Box?" The kids looked at each other. They didn't know. "Hope," said Mrs. Q.

Everyone thought about this for a long moment, then Billy said, "I guess we'd better get as much hope out of this thing as we can—while we can."

"So, you're on board?" the General asked both kids.

Billy wanted to say "yes," but his invention was different from dynamite or $E=mc^2$. He wrestled with some thoughts until finally he could put voice to them. "I won't use it to kill anyone," he said. "This is magic. Magic has to be better than that."

"Understood," said General Quinofski. "I hope you're right." Then he turned to his daughter, "Suzy?"

"Sure, I guess."

"Good," said the General as he stood up and got his jacket, "because we're going to have to start right way."

Building an entire new Research and Development unit around a couple of 12-year-olds is not the hardest thing the Army Corp of Engineers has ever done, but they might have thought it was the silliest. Once the kids agreed to help, Suzy's Dad stayed on the phone to the Pentagon the rest of the day ordering a lot of people around. One of those orders was to the base hospital. He wanted to make sure the kids hadn't suffered any ill-effects from the wand. So Dr. Mead poked, prodded, and bled them. Suzy finally got to a see a scan of her own brain, but by the time that happened, she was so tired of having tests done that she didn't care that much.

Once Dr. Mead pronounced them perfectly normal, the kids met back with the General at Suzy's house. Between calls, e-mails and text messages he informed them they were now employed by the United States government with top secret clearance on project Hocus Pocus.

"Okay," said Suzy, "but only if you promise to give it a better name."

"And never send us to the doctor again," said Billy.

The General let their comments pass. "This means you cannot tell anyone the truth about what happened. It was just an elaborate trick."

This was a hard pill for Billy to swallow. He had humiliated himself in front of the whole school, and now he couldn't tell anyone what he'd really done? "Oh… great…"

It wasn't hard for the General to pick up on Billy's thoughts. "The world will know the truth soon enough, Billy, don't you worry about that."

"I guess…"

"Go home," he told Billy. "Sleep. Meet us back here in the morning. We've got work to get done before you two head back to school on Monday."

"Fine," said Billy. "See you here in the morning."

"Billy, wait up," said Suzy. "I'll walk you home."

It was the first quiet time they'd had together since he disappeared. Even so, Billy didn't feel like they were alone, since Fame trotted along beside him. There was one way to resolve that issue.

"Suzy, can you keep a secret?"

"For the safety of the United States and possibly everyone on the planet, I should hope so."

"Even from your Dad?"

Suzy walked a few steps before answering. "Would depend on the secret."

"The thing is… I keep coming back to what the old wizard told me, 'from now on, you're not paranoid.' I don't know who I can trust or who I can talk to, except you."

"Yeah, well, hasn't it always been that way?"

"Exactly."

"So what's the secret?"

"My cat's not really a cat."

Billy! said Fame loudly inside his head.

"Hush, Fame." That was out loud.

"She didn't say anything, Billy."

"Yes she did. Inside my head."

"Are you *sure* you're not paranoid?"

"Fame," said Billy, "show Suzy your human form."

Are you sure you know what you're doing? asked Fame, only this time, Suzy heard her, too.

"Was that her?"

Billy ignored Suzy and answered the question. "She's just as responsible for making the wand as I am, so there's no reason why we can't share you."

"Share her? What are you talking about, Billy?"

"She's a familiar," he told Suzy. "As in a witch's familiar. She's like a servant."

"I prefer 'assistant,'" said the now human Fame, in her tomboy clothes.

"Holy!" Suzy cut herself off with her own surprise. "How did you do that?"

"Kind of like the way Billy made brunch, only different."

Suzy suddenly remembered. "Ew! You licked my feet!"

"I licked syrup off your feet," Fame corrected. "And I was a cat. That's what cats do."

Billy was a bit behind the curve of the conversation, but wanted to get it back on track. "Suzy, meet Fame. Fame, Suzy."

"We met before," said Suzy.

"Yeah, but not as humans," said Billy.

"I'm still not human, but it's nice to meet you again, Suzy."

Suzy finally gave into social graces. "Nice to meet you, too." She offered her hand, and Fame shook it, which got another reaction. "Oh, that's freaky."

"Yeah, I'm more energy than matter. Touching can feel strange."

"You feel like all cat's fur, no cat."

"I never thought of it that way, but it's good reason for my animal form, huh?"

"Yeah."

With his two friends getting along, Billy pushed forward. "Okay, cards on the table. Trust is currency. Suzy I've known most of my life and trust with my life. Fame, we've just met, but you've not given me any reason not to trust you, and you can read my thoughts—so I don't have a lot of choice in the matter."

"You do," said Fame, "but I understand your point. It's well taken."

"Good. You should regard Suzy and I as equals."

"I can't exactly do that. The wand has your DNA in it, so I take orders from you."

"Well, then, my order is to treat Suzy as you would me."

Fame turned to her new friend, "You understand that if there's a conflict…"

"…then we girls are sticking together, right?"

"We understand each other, fine!" said Fame as the two young women shared a conspiratorial smile.

"All right," said the boy in the group. "We're a team, then? All three of us."

"All for one," said Fame.

"And one for all."

By this time, they'd reached Billy's trailer. The closer they got to the front door, the more sullen Billy became. When he stepped up onto the porch, Fame changed back into a cat, and Billy stared at the knob.

"Billy," said Suzy. "Isn't this why you wanted a wand in the first place? Make your wish—your big wish—and open the door."

He almost smiled as he took his wand out of his pocket. He didn't need a word to focus his thoughts. He'd pictured this so many times before that the image was crystal clear: a clean home. He savored the feeling for a moment, then pressed the button on his wand.

Pop. No big explosion. No white flash. Just a tiny pop of energy escaping from the stick.

"Did it work?" Suzy asked.

"Don't know. Let's see." Billy tried the door. It opened all the way without a struggle. Inside, the trailer was immaculate. His mother, passed out in her chair, didn't notice a thing.

Nice place, said Fame to both of them as she bounded inside and preceded to scratch the fresh, new carpet.

"That was a good one, Billy."

"Yeah," he said. "I hope they're all like that."

Sixteen

Someone Old, Something New

A HORRIBLE WAIL WOKE Billy from a sound sleep. At first he thought a cat had been hit by a car or something. Then he thought one of the neighbors kids might have been killed, and the howling came from a distraught mother.

"My stuff!"

Well, he was half right. It was the cries of a mother in distress... his.

"What happened to my things?" she sobbed.

Billy checked the clock on his computer. Two in the morning.

"Why? Why? Why?" Obviously, she'd come to and wasn't happy with the spotless, trashless, trailer.

Billy crawled out of bed to find his mother splayed out on the floor. "What did you do with my stuff?"

"It wasn't stuff, Mom, it was trash."

"Maybe to you, but not to me!" She cried like a baby.

"Mom… Mom!"

"Where is my stuff?" she said between sobs.

"I don't know, Mom." Not a good answer. She bellowed tears. "I didn't get rid of anything that has sentimental value. It's all here, Mom."

"No, it's not."

"It is. It's been put away."

"Where?"

"In drawers. In closets. Wherever it could fit. The rest was trash."

"No, it wasn't! It was my treasure."

"Mom…"

"Where are my newspapers?"

"You mean the ones that you had already clipped the coupons out of?"

"Yes. Where are they?" She could have been the only survivor of a plane crash full of children the way she couldn't stop crying. If Billy hadn't lived with her mess for so long, she would have broken his heart. Instead, she was making him mad.

"Gone, Mom. Your newspapers with rectangular holes cut out of them are gone."

"I want them back."

"Well, you can't have them back. They don't exist anymore."

"I hate you," she said with a red, puffy face soaked in tears.

Just then Peter got home. In all the commotion Billy

hadn't heard him drive up, which is saying something considering the decibels his car generated. "What's going on?" he asked before he even got inside. "I can hear you two all the way down the street." Then he opened the door. "Wow."

"Billy took my stuff."

"Good," was all Peter said.

"Make him give it back!"

Billy finally snapped, "Mom, shut-up!" She didn't, but neither did he. "I know you're sick. I know you have something wrong with your brain that makes you live like a pig, but you know what? I don't."

"Me neither," said Peter.

"You want your stuff. You think you can't live without your piles of trash, but I can't live with them. I could bring all of that crap back to make you happy, but it wouldn't make *me* happy."

"Me neither," said Peter again.

"Right," said Billy. "We live here, too, you know? And we are a lot more important than your stuff. So you're going to have to get over it, Mom!"

Billy had thrown plenty of temper tantrums as a child, but as he stormed off to his room and slammed the door behind him, he got the feeling that he hadn't lost his temper, he'd used it. His emotions were not out of control. They flowed in a way that made him comprehend the saying, "righteous anger."

He had about two seconds to make this insight, since the old man from the Quantum World was sitting in his desk chair.

"What?" asked Billy, still a little hot. "Are you here to make me go apologize?"

The old guy shook his head a little and calmly said, "no."

"Fame called you 'The Teacher.' Are you here to teach me how even good magic can bring pain and sorrow?"

"Do I need to?"

"Not if you know the way her crying makes me feel inside," said Billy. His anger subsided. He gave into the heartbreak of seeing his mother in such pain. He slumped onto his bed and tears began to flow. "Why does she have to be…?" He picked up his wand from the bedside table and held it up to the old wizard, "Teach me how to make her not crazy."

The man pursed his lips, stood, and paced the small room for a bit, stopping in front of the window. "You think she is crazy because she says the gnomes are spying on her?"

"Among other things, yeah."

"Look outside."

Billy did, and sure enough, four or five gnomes were hiding in the grass and behind trees. These weren't ceramic statues. They were living creatures. They signaled to each other as they stalked the house. When they got close enough, the Teacher said, "Boo!" and they scattered like cockroaches.

"Your friend Suzy was right about mental disorders and the Quantum World. What did your mother say in the hospital?"

"I don't know. She was screaming like a lunatic."

"She was screaming, yes, but 'like a lunatic' is your interpretation. What did she actually say?"

"Um… I don't remember exactly. Something about not letting them take her baby."

"Meaning you."

"Yes. That, and I shouldn't do what they say—whoever 'they' are."

"At the hospital, what did the other patients say to you? What did they tell you to do?"

"Nothing. They were all …"

"Crazy? What did they tell you to do?"

"They told me to break the connection. Break the connection and make all things possible."

The old man gave him a knowing look and said, "Maybe you should have listened to your mother."

"So… Mom is right? The gnomes really are spies who report back to evil creatures that want to kidnap me?"

"Yes and no. Your mother's imagination created the gnomes to personify the creatures that her mind knows are there but can't identify."

"How do I know that you're not a figment of *my* imagination?" asked Billy.

"You don't. Because I am. Well, yours and about every other person's in Western Civilization dating back to before Abraham's time. I have been the wise old father-teacher since the first poor human wondered who his or her father might be."

"Wow, so you really are old."

"Benefits of the collective consciousness. Children's imaginary friends aren't so lucky."

"You mean the monsters under my bed were real?"

"As long as you believed in them, yes."

"Wait a minute. We create you? I thought it was the other way around, that life couldn't exist without you guys."

"Chicken and the egg, Billy. Or, if you prefer, the paradox of discovery. No matter how much you learn about the mysteries of life, there is always a little bit more."

Billy set that thought aside to get back to the subject at hand. "So, Mom can see those gnomes?"

"Oh, yes. We've always had a strange symbiotic relationship, your world and mine. Normally, neither side is aware of the other, but some individuals—like those people in the hospital—become enlightened. They are branded as either lunatics or prophets without rhyme or reason as to why one is sage and the other psychotic."

"So Mom can see both worlds?"

"Apparently so."

"Could I use my wand to make her see just ours?"

"I don't know, Billy. I really don't." His attention drifted for a moment. Then he smiled. "It's not often I get to say that." He clapped his hands and shifted his attention back to Billy. "Your wand is something new, Billy, and I'm a very old consciousness. I'm looking forward to seeing how it all turns out." The Teacher stepped toward the door like he was leaving.

"Yeah, me too," said Billy.

"I almost forgot. I came here to warn you. Your wand is as much treasured on my side of the divide as it is on yours. Certain factions have taken steps to lure you into a trap."

"What kind of a trap?"

"If I knew that, they wouldn't be such a threat, would they?"

"I suppose not."

"You'll see it coming. You will know it's a trap, yet you'll walk right into it."

"Why would I do that?"

"They are good at what they do… so you have to be better, Billy."

"How?"

"I don't know for sure. They've beaten me on so many occasions."

"Who are they?"

"They are us. In your world that's a philosophical distinction, not so in mine. But that's a topic for another time. For now, let's just call them 'they.'"

"You're starting to sound as crazy as my Mom."

"What did I say about crazy? It's a matter of perspective." The old man held Billy's gaze to make sure the lesson sank in. Billy nodded. The Teacher continued. "They have ways of manipulating an individual, or entire populations, without you ever noticing."

"Like the patients at the hospital."

"Very good. Who else?"

"What do you mean? They're the only crazy people… I mean, the only—what do I call them?"

"How about 'Influenced'?"

"Okay, so they are the only 'Influenced' People I've seen."

"The people at the hospital are highly influenced. Others might seem perfectly normal, but suddenly find they have a compulsion to do something out of the ordinary.

For you, there are no more coincidences. Everything that happens to you will be for a reason—a reason you might not see, but should always be on the lookout for."

"They manipulated me into making this wand."

"Since before you were even born, Billy. They are patient beings."

"So my wand is evil?"

Again, the old man smiled. Billy was learning to hate that teaching method. "Your wand is an inanimate object, a tool. Good and evil are in your heart, and only you can determine which will have access to your actions."

"But they manipulated me. They helped me make the wand. Why would they do that?"

"I'm not sure. They may not even know themselves. They might have just been mucking about to see what kind of trouble they could start up."

"Trouble?"

"They like chaos. It sparks human imagination, which is what they are really after."

"Who have they trapped before?"

"King Arthur for one."

"I thought he was fictitious."

"What you know about him is mostly fiction, sure—but the truth at the heart of the legend is what's important. That chaos sparked the creation of a whole new fictitious world."

"Fame said you were Merlin."

"Guilty as charged," said … Merlin. "Arthur saw into the Quantum World and was called a prophet. He learned that reason was more powerful than force, that intellect could bring stability. He did not see how love, jealousy, and lust could overpower reason."

"And that's how they trapped him."

"And that's how they trapped him," repeated Merlin, the Teacher.

Billy was perplexed. "But... I *like* the stories of King Author."

"Thank you. It took centuries of hard work to turn wars of darkness into the dream Arthur envisioned." The old man's eyes drifted off for a moment, leaving Billy to wonder what it would be like to carry around so many memories. "They got Harry Truman..." His memories must have been moving forward in time. "...without him even knowing they existed. They whittled his options down to two choices: lose tens of thousands—possibly hundreds of thousands—of lives on both sides in a long drawn out invasion of Japan, or drop a bomb that would change the world forever."

"How would that stir up imagination?"

"Paranoia. Fear. They love all those imagined enemies."

"And now they're after me?" said Billy.

"And now they're after you."

"But, I thought imagination was a good thing. That's what they always tell us in school."

"Oh," said Merlin, "it is." He took Billy by the shoulders and looked into him with the kindest, most caring eyes a person could ever wish to have cast upon them. "Imagination is the most wonderful thing in the universe. It is Manna from Heaven."

"So...?"

"Like anything good, in the wrong hands, it can be just as horrible."

Billy's wand had taught him that dilemma well. "Have you ever beaten them?"

"Oh, yes. We've each had our victories, but they don't last."

"Any advice?" asked Billy.

"Yes," said Merlin. "Think of something new."

Seventeen

Sunday School

"THAT'S IT?" ASKED SUZY when Billy filled her in the next morning. "He's the greatest teacher of all time and that's all the advice he gives you?"

"That's it," said Billy before letting out a full yawn. His mother hadn't stopped her noise until just before he had to get up to walk over to Suzy's for the operation Hocus Pocus Sunday morning meeting. He flopped on the couch in her basement while she ate cereal and they waited for her father to come downstairs.

The Teacher is not the kind of person who tells you what to do, said Fame inside the heads of her two clients. *He knows that any idea you come up with will be a thousand times stronger than trying to "re-image" his thoughts.*

"That's assuming we come up with an idea at all," said Billy.

Fame curled up on the cushion of a rocking chair in the corner to join Billy in a nap. *Yeah, well, that's not my problem.*

Before Suzy could think of a good zinger for the uppity cat, her father came downstairs.

"So, I talked with your principal," he said before so much as a "Hello" or "Did you sleep okay?"

"Good morning, Daddy," was Suzy's subtle reminder for him to be civil.

"I'm sorry, kids. Good morning." He gave his daughter a kiss, then noticed, "You look tired, Billy."

"Long night."

"Anything I should know?"

Billy glanced to Suzy. They both checked in with Fame. *Your call, Billy*, she thought.

"No," Billy finally said to the General. "Personal stuff."

"Okay… but son, you're my Michael Jordon. I need you focused."

"Who?"

General Quinofski gave Billy a look that said, *really!?* Billy gave it right back to him. "Never mind," said the older of the two. "The point is, if you need anything—I mean from a toothbrush to a Lamborghini, you let me know."

"Sir," said Billy, "I have a magic wand. If I need anything like that, I can pull it out of thin air."

What he did need was an idea about how to handle the mysterious trap that lay ahead of him. "I tell you what, though, sir. I'll teach you all I know about magic wands, if you teach me about military strategy."

"That's a deal."

Fame relayed a mental message. *Suzy said to tell you that you're not going to find any new ideas from military school.*

Tell her that new ideas come from old ones, he thought, then heard Fame quote him verbatim.

She said talking this way is really weird.

Add it to the list, thought Billy.

"As I was saying, I talked to your principal."

That's a phrase that has sent chills down the spines of many a kid on any given day, but not Billy and Suzy. For them it usually meant they were going to get an award or go on another convention for smart kids, so the lumps of fear in their throats were a whole new experience.

The General didn't notice their apprehension. "I tried to talk him into a suspension."

"A suspension!?" Billy was mortified.

"Dad! You can't let him do that."

"I was trying to talk him into three days."

"But, Dad... suspension? That's... that's..." She couldn't put it into words. School was all either one of them had in their lives. No matter what, there was always school. The place where they shined.

"There goes my perfect attendance record," said Billy.

"Mine, too."

You guys are pathetic, thought Fame. *Absolutely no sense of adventure.*

"Wait a minute," said Billy. "You said you *tried* to talk him into a three day suspension? Does that mean we've been expelled!?"

"Dad!"

"Heck, kids, I *wanted* him to expel you. It's not like you're going to need college or any kind of formal education once your invention goes public, and I could use you on this project 24/7, but Mr. Dillon insisted that all be forgiven. I couldn't very well argue the point without filling him in our secret."

"So, we're going to school tomorrow?" Suzy asked.

"Yes. And that means you don't say a word about the wand, you understand me?"

"Yes, sir," they moaned together.

"It was a trick that went wrong, right?"

Again, together, "Yes, sir." They both had issues with explaining the goings on of last Friday. Billy about the explosion and disappearance. Suzy about being taken away in handcuffs.

The General wasn't entirely numb to the social plight of his daughter and her friend, but there wasn't anything he could do to help their situation beyond keeping them busy. "The order of the day is to get our engineers up and running so they can work while you're in school tomorrow. Think you're ready for it?"

"Briefing engineers and scientists, oh yeah," said Billy. "Facing the kids at school—not so much."

The General had a driver waiting outside. He took the three of them to an abandoned area on the far side of the base. Nature had started to reclaim her territory from the concrete, brick, and mortar that made up the barracks of old. Grass, weeds, and small vermin staked claims wherever they could get a foothold and were surprised by the sudden influx of human activity. Billy and Suzy were taken aback as well. Trucks dominated the place. The ones that weren't being unloaded, hustled back to the airbase for more of the crates, boxes, furniture, computers, and other stuff being hauled by exhausted 18-year-old recruits who seemed as awestruck by this special weekend assignment as everyone else. Hummers ferried VIP-looking people to the site, then sped away between the trucks.

General Quinofski was out of the car before it came to a stop. "Ladies and gentlemen," he said to get the attention of the one or two people who didn't notice his arrival. "If you have a rank of colonel or above, or an advanced degree in one of our various specialty subjects, I need you inside the building. If not, you have a thirty minute break for chow—and I do mean thirty minutes, so get a move on."

The enlisted all scrambled for the nearest vehicle, since it was probably a thirty minute walk to the cafeteria from this remote corner of the base. Suzy's Dad stopped one of them. "Sergeant, take a detail and get some coffee going. Order up those fru-fru breakfast snacks for our guests from the academic world."

"Already done, sir. The kitchen is set up in the back."

The General dismissed him with, "You're a good man," then said in the direction of his car, "Kids! Let's go. We haven't got all day."

Soldier and scientist alike stopped for a second as if to collectively ask, "did I hear what I thought I heard?" All eyes turned to the General's Humvee, as Billy and Suzy stepped onto the scene.

"No, I don't feel awkward at all," said Suzy out of the side of her mouth. "My Daddy just overnighted me an entire research department and set it up in my backyard."

"Let's go," ordered the aforementioned Daddy—which was also a command for everyone to get back to what they were doing.

Inside was worse. Billy recognized some of the faces staring at him. He'd seen them in *Scientific American* magazine, on *Nova*, and the Discovery Science Channel. They were his heroes. The top quantum physics minds in the world.

"I know it's a mess," said Quinofski, "but if I can have your attention. Feel free to have a seat if you can find something that'll hold your weight."

He paused while everyone settled among the crates, boxes, packing material, and unassembled equipment that occupied the room.

"None of you knows why you're here, so you can quit asking each other. You're all about to find out. Once you do, it stays in the room. Do I make myself clear?"

"HOO-AH!" said the soldiers, loud enough to make those in white lab coats jump.

"For all you civilians, that means yes. What you are about to see is top secret. Did anyone not sign-off on the government non-disclosure forms you were given?" He held up a form he'd pulled from his briefcase. "No? Everyone understands the importance of this, yes? Good." He turned to the kids, "Billy, Suzy," and waved them over to his side. "This young physics genius is Billy Bobble. The young lady is his equal in biology. She is also my daughter, Suzy Quinofski."

A subtle ripple of doubt coursed through the room. Did a United States General just move mountains to present his daughter's sixth-grade science project?

The General expected it. "Billy. We are not going to have any respect or attention from the people in this room without a demonstration."

"Yes, sir" Billy mumbled. He was nervous. How many times had he dreamed of giving a presentation of his work before the very people in that room? But he always thought he'd have a little more time to prepare—like a decade or two. Even an hour would have been nice. Suddenly, he felt like he was standing before his heroes in his underwear. His dreams and nightmares were coming true at the same time. The wand shook terribly in his hand. "What should I do, sir?"

"Something simple, son. Whatever you think you can do and do well."

"I've gotten pretty good at cleaning up," he said.

"That sounds like a good idea. Everyone… if you could stand up, and… Billy? Do we need to move out of the way?"

He thought of his mother sleeping in the middle of the living room last night. "I don't think so."

"Fine. Have at it, son."

In his head Billy pictured everything in the room. He had to find the right word. *Banish*? Banish what? He developed a mental image about the function and all the stuff. What to keep and what to banish? It was easy with his mom's junk. He'd been thinking of the answer to that question for as long as he could remember. Here, he made four categories in his head: Permanent structures (the building, doors, floors, etc.), what had been needed to get stuff here (packing materials and such), what would be needed moving forward (the equipment), and people. Then he pictured all but the second category staying exactly where it was. The rest he would banish into nothingness.

Wait!

"Do you need the packing slips?" he asked the General.

The whole room laughed. As they did, he saw Fame slip in through an open window in the back. In his mind, he changed his last grouping from "people" to "all living things."

"I suppose we should keep the packing slips," the General said.

Billy imagined them now as things not only needed to get stuff here, but as necessary items moving forward. The degree to which he did not want to screw this up was OTC. Off The Chart.

He closed his eyes, took a deep breath and thought, *keep what is necessary, banish the rest,* and with a flourish hit the button on his wand.

Nothing happened.

Silence. He opened his eyes. At first everyone was dumbstruck, then they shifted their weight, mumbled to each other, and worst of all looked sympathetic toward Billy and Suzy.

"I don't know what's wrong," said Billy.

"It's all right, son, I've seen this sort of thing happen before. We need a minute…"

As he continued to talk, Billy panicked, *What happened, Fame? Why didn't it work?*

Don't ask me, she said, *I'm just a being from the Quantum World, I don't know anything about your mechanical magic wand.*

"What's it supposed to do?" asked someone from the

crowd. Billy thought he recognized the voice from a Discovery Channel show.

"It disassociates Time from Space," said Billy.

"Are you insane?" asked another physicist. Then they all busted out in loud discussions.

"That's not possible."

"Even if it were possible—why would you want to do it?"

"It would destroy the fabric of the universe."

"No," said Billy. "DNA locks all living things in linear Time."

"What's DNA got to do with anything?" came a response from another side of the room. Whoever said that got dirty looks from Suzy and a collection of people Billy assumed to be biologists. "In a quantum sense, I mean," said the heckler. That put everyone into heaps of discussion. They paid absolutely no attention to Billy, who was trying to defend his theories against unanimous dissent from this collection of the few people on the planet who could really understand it. Suddenly, the ridicule he was sure to face at school didn't seem so bad. He was about to be laughed out of the scientific community forever.

Then Suzy whispered in his ear, "did you check the battery?"

Billy's eyes lit up. How stupid could he be? Quickly, he popped the back of the wand open, pulled out the double-A and checked the indicator. Dead. He showed it to Suzy and her dad. The General took it. "Colonel," he shouted over the din to a man in a beret near the door, and tossed the battery to him. "I need a fresh one, on the double."

"Yes, sir!"

The General turned back to the kids. "That's going to be one for the history books."

But Billy didn't see the irony. Nothing had changed in his life. He was laughed at in kindergarten by his peers, and now was being laughed at by his heroes.

Suzy had seen this look on her friend's face many times before. Often, like now, she'd shared it. "It's okay, Billy." She was talking as much to herself as to him.

"Son," said the General, pointing to the gaggle of geeks arguing among themselves, "you understand all that gibberish?"

"Yeah," said Billy to the second button on his shirt. "They're saying I'm crazy."

"Well, if you're crazy, then what am I for believing in you?" The General was interrupted by the returning Colonel, who tossed him a new battery. He held it up to Billy. "Load and lock, kid."

Billy took the battery, shoved it into his wand, and waited for his orders. The General looked over the crowd. About thirty civilians were all in heated discussions. Around them were five special operations officers who stood at ease staring straight ahead. "Fire when ready," he said to Billy.

Billy didn't give it as much thought as he had earlier. He simply pictured the room as it would be tomorrow if everything went as planned, pressed the button on his wand and found himself in the middle of what looked, sounded, felt, smelled, and even tasted like everything in the universe. The combination of everything that ever was, would be, might have been, or might be was so incomprehensible that Billy's brain kind of shut down all of his senses—so everything became exactly like nothing.

Into this extremely strange existence strolled Fame, in her human form, dressed like a general. At the same time, she wasn't there at all, so Billy had a hard time talking to her.

"Where am I?"

"You're in my world now, Billy," said Fame in her best Quinofski imitation. "Or, really, you're in a passage between your world and mine, but it works more like mine than yours."

"At least it's quiet here. I messed up something terrible." With the feeling of screwing up, came input from Billy's senses. Swirling horribleness threatened to engulf him.

"Billy, focus!" said Fame. "You're here for a reason."

"What?" The tide of torture ebbed.

"You have to keep your mind clear and focused, okay? You don't want to stay here long, or you'll never leave. What did you want to accomplish?"

"I want the room and equipment to be all set up and ready to go." As Billy thought of the barracks, the horror of his self-doubt faded, replaced by endless input in the colors, textures, etc. of the room he still stood in, somewhere in the universe."

"Okay," said Fame like she knew exactly what to do. "I have no idea how to do that."

"Can I move stuff around myself?"

"Why would you want to do that?"

"I want to open the boxes, set up the stuff, clean up, you know. Make it look like it is supposed to look when all the work is done."

"Why not just think it that way and be done with it?"

"Because I didn't know I could do that!"

"Well, I'm not sure you can, either!"

They were shouting. Experiencing all of everything like that can make for short tempers.

"I'll give it a try." With his mind—or his actual free hand, he wasn't sure—Billy grabbed onto a future moment in Time when everything was set up, and dragged it to his current physical space. His brain then strained against the chaos that is the Quantum World to imagine himself back in the exact moment of Time and place in Space when he'd pressed the button, and with all his might told his finger to let go.

When he could once again focus on his surroundings, he saw the explosion of white energy flashing out from all directions around his wand. Everything moved in slow motion inside his head, though he knew he was back in real time. In the wake of the energy that moved through the room, Billy saw the materials change from the way they are now to the way they would be tomorrow. The people were unaffected—except, of course, if they happened to be sitting or leaning on something that was no longer there, or pushed out of the way by something that suddenly was. The force of the atmosphere, either filling voids or being displaced, made sonic booms around the room.

Followed immediately by stunned silence. The only ones not surprised where Billy, Suzy, her father, and Fame, who was once again a cat. The rest were literally struck dumb. Not a single thought came to the heads of all those great minds. The soldiers, who no doubt witnessed things no civilian could imagine, had seen nothing like this. In less than a second, the room had gone from a shambles to clean and functional. The power was on. All of the equipment was set up, plugged in, and ready to use. The floors had been swept, mopped, and polished. Stuff that hadn't arrived yet was not only there, but in place, as if by…

The General broke the silence. "As I said people, Top Secret."

And then there erupted thunderous applause. Billy grinned at Suzy, and she smiled back. Their joy busted out as laughter. They hugged each other as they never had before. The scientists all rushed up to pat them on the back and see the extraordinary invention. It was the happiest moment of their young lives.

General Quinofski had not risen to his level of command without knowing people and how to manage them. He let the kids have their moment in the sun. He let the scientists have their informal question and answer session without interruption. He let himself enjoy the moment as a proud father. After a few minutes of this he announced that coffee and pastries were in the back for anyone interested.

They soon discovered the coffee was cold, the pastries stale, and the cream curdled. Quinofski was about to have the stripes of a certain sergeant who told him this was set up fresh, when Billy interrupted. "That might be my fault, Sir. I pulled the equipment from … how do I describe it? … an ideal tomorrow… of all the billions of possible tomorrows there are." A murmur of respect came from the scientists. "So, I guess, that stuff had been sitting out for 24 hours … somewhere in the Quantum World."

The scientists chuckled, and soon found the stale

sweetbreads and cream the most interesting thing they'd ever seen. The military men and women just wanted hot caffeine. "Can you bring it back?" asked one of them.

"Yes, do!" said a scientist.

"Bring it back! Bring it back!" they soon chanted.

Like a performer pretending to wave off a request for an encore, Billy humbly asked, "Just the coffee and stuff, right? Not the crates and things?"

The collective intellectuals cheered like kids at a birthday party.

"All right, give me some room."

"You're incorrigible," Suzy said as she walked past, but she had a big grin on her face.

Tell me about it, said Fame to her two secret friends. She had jumped onto an x-ray machine for a better view.

"Look, it's Schrödinger's Cat," said one of the less-than-imaginative physicists.

If only he knew, said Fame with a mental giggle. *Time to use your favorite magic word.*

"What's that?" asked Suzy.

Billy raised his wand, said "Oops," and pushed the button.

FLASH! The coffee was hot, the cream was cold, the food fresh, and the scientists delighted.

It took about ten minutes for the quality of conversation to devolve to the paradoxical genius of the *Bill and Ted's Excellent Adventure* movie, at which point General Quinofski called the meeting back to order.

"Ladies and gentlemen, I don't have time to discuss with you the long history of cooperation that the military has shared with science. From the Ancient Greeks and Egyptians, to da Vinci, the Wright Brothers, and so on."

"Oppenheimer," offered one of the civilians with an unflattering tone in his voice.

"Yes," said the General, "Robert Oppenheimer."

"Who's he?" Suzy whispered to Billy. They were now sitting with the scientists.

Tell her, thought Billy to Fame, *the physicist most responsible for building the atom bomb.*

"Mengele," said another Ph.D.

Nazi biologist, Billy thought right away.

She says, 'He was no biologist. He was a monster.'

"Like I said, I don't have time to discuss it. We have an incident." The serious tone of his voice stopped all conversation. "A special forces unit under my command by order of both this and the previous president's administration has been in operation in the Kashmir region between India and Pakistan. Another thing I don't have time to discuss is the long history of hatred and war between the Muslims, now in Pakistan, and Hindus in India. Suffice to say, they don't like each other, and they both have nuclear weapons. Their current excuse for a reason to consider using them is the god-forsaken land of Kashmir where our special ops soldiers were in support of a CIA mission to win friends and influence people. A squad has been captured by extremists from one side or the other—and for the record, I don't particularly favor either. Off the record, I think they are all a bunch of bloodthirsty lunatics and I wish we could rid the whole world of their childish, selfish, cry-baby violence."

He took a second to collect himself, then joked, "Could you do that for us, Billy?"

No one laughed.

"I think that's a little beyond my power, sir," he said.

"Good," said the General. "No one person should have that kind of power. We'd have more than stale pastries and curdled milk to deal with, huh?"

"Hoo-Ah!" said the soldiers.

"So, the mission is to find where they are being held and get our soldiers back before the enemy can use them in a dog and pony show to bring about the nuclear Armageddon so many religious nuts constantly pray for."

This is the trap, thought Billy. Fame didn't need to relay the message to Suzy. The look she gave him said they were both thinking the same thing.

"I have no intention of sending a 12-year-old boy into harm's way, so you scientists are here to make wands for a squad of soldiers that'll get my people back, and quite possibly save the human race from total nuclear annihilation." He let the purpose for their gathering hang in the air, then, "My guess is we have about a week before the captives start doing unpleasant things. After we're done, I will happily share a drink with you and discuss Oppenheimer's dilemma until the wee hours. Until then, we have work to do."

One of the scientists in the back asked, "Why can't Billy just zap the soldiers from there to here?"

"We're not sure where 'there' is exactly," said the General.

Another scientist asked, "Once we do know where they are, why not have Billy send these soldiers over to rescue them?"

"That may be our only option, but I'd much rather have soldiers armed with magic than bullets. These extremists want to draw us into a fight in the disputed region so they can point to the bad ole United States and scale up an international incident."

"Like scared bullies," said Billy. "The ones that want you to throw the first punch so they don't get in trouble."

"That's exactly right," said the General. "The trouble is, if the teachers don't stop this fight it could go nuclear. With a little magic on our side, we might avoid throwing any punches at all."

But the magic is exactly what they're after, thought Billy.

The day was too short for the kids. For the first time in their lives they were working with people who not only understood what they were saying, but got their jokes. They split into two teams. On one side of the barracks-turned-laboratory, the same physicists who chastised Billy for purposely creating a Cartesian product between two infinite sets, now praised him for his bold ingenuity. On the other side of the room, Suzy's combination of enzymes and nucleotides to manipulate introns without splicing was creating quite a stir.

Together with the military officers, they watched the basement video of the wand in action. First in real time, then frame-by-frame as the white energy burst from the stick.

"What is that?" asked a biologist.

"We think it might be Bose-Einstein condensate," said Billy. "It's extremely cold."

"It's blowing out of the wand like a grenade," said an officer. "I bet if you drilled a hole in the end of it, you could focus that energy on the target."

"Like a laser," said a scientist.

Discussions went around the room about the similarities between a lasing tube and Billy's Magnetic Field Imploder, as he called it. They decided the hole in the tip of the wand wouldn't be drilled into the wood, but instead would be a point of weakness in the magnetic field where energy could escape. Billy understood the concept—like the ½-mirrored side of a laser—but he couldn't get his mind off what the soldier had said: "…focus on the target."

Billy felt Suzy's stare and knew they were thinking the same thing. Their little afterschool hobby was about to become a major new tool in the US military arsenal whether they liked it or not.

Eighteen

The Curse of the Coven

THE DAY ENDED WITH a heated discussion about what to do with the wand while Billy was in school on Monday. The adults all wanted to study it—and fix the tip to focus the energy. Fame didn't like that idea.

You need your wand, Billy. You can never be without it, she said to both her hosts.

I'll be fine. Truth be told, he didn't like the idea of having the thing with him in school. *The wand is what they are after. Why do you think Dillon didn't suspend us? I think they've been controlling him for a while now.*

That was a powerful argument. Fame gave in, but she swore to protect him. *One sign of trouble and I'm jumping across Time and Space to bring you your wand.*

Good to know.

The next morning, Billy and Suzy passed a gauntlet

of stares to get into school, Suzy tried to keep them on message. "We have to focus. Those soldiers in Kashmir are obviously the trap."

"I don't know," said Billy. "The Teacher said I would knowingly walk into it. I can't see myself going to Kashmir no matter what."

"Still," said Suzy, as she turned away from Billy to go to her class, "it is the trap."

"Of course it is. See you at lunch."

"Mr. Bobble," boomed the voice of Mrs. McClain, his English teacher, as he walked into her room. "What... is *that*?" She was pointing to Fame, who had come into class right behind him.

You want me to tell her? Fame said only to Billy.

"No!" he said to the animal.

"Bobble...?"

"It's a cat," he said in answer to her first question.

Mrs. McClain looked over her glasses and the giggles of the students already in their seats. "I can see that, Mr. Bobble. What is it doing in my class?"

Well, thought Fame, *since Billy had to leave his wand with the research scientists...*

"Uh..." said Billy. He found it very hard to concentrate on the dressing down by the teacher of his worst subject with the thoughts of a sarcastic cat from an alternate universe in his head.

And since psychotic beings of unimaginable determination want to do who knows what with Billy's brain...

"She's ah…"

I thought it best to—

"…a stray."

A STRAY!? Billy, I'm hurt.

"Shut-up!"

"I beg your pardon?" Apparently, Mrs. McClain thought the last comment was directed at her.

"I was talking to the cat."

"As long as the cat doesn't start talking back."

Oh, pleeeeeeeeease let me say something!

"No! … Ma'am… the cat doesn't talk."

But oh, how the class could laugh.

"Then it has no business in an English class, does it? Send it into the hall at least."

"Go," said Billy.

Fame turned up her nose, walked out of the classroom, then as a group of students came in she tucked behind them, transformed into her human guise and took a desk next to Billy's.

"And you are?" Mrs. McClain now focused on the new face before her.

Transfer student, thought Billy, then, *No! Foreign exchange.*

That's not even a lie, Fame thought. She then said, "Bonjour. Mon nom est Fame. Je suis une étudiante de Paris en échange."

"Ah… Bon fromage," said Mrs. McClain, trying out her French. "Nous sommes heureux ainsi de vous avoir à notre étable."

Fame could hardly contain herself. *She wished me 'good cheese,'* she told Billy, who about blew snot out of his nose in holding back the sudden laugh. *And she's welcoming me to her cowshed.*

And so Fame became the school's latest exchange student from Paris, which took some of the spotlight off Billy and Suzy.

That is, until lunch.

Oh, the drama.

The players were in their fair weather places around the courtyard. The cheerleaders and socially gifted girls were at the tables near the door where they could pass judgment on all who paraded by. The jocks were in the middle where everyone was within easy soda-can-throwing distance. The freaks were out on the grass at the open end of the three-sided yard, and the non-allied kids were interspersed throughout the place.

But all eyes were on two tables: the Geeks about halfway down the long side of the building, and the Witches of Winston High in the middle of the short wall furthest from the door. Billy put on a good show the last time they gathered. Rumors had been flying over the weekend about what kind of payback the Witches had in mind.

"Zer are weak minds here, BillEE," said Fame as she sat down with Billy and Suzy at the Geek's table.

"Weak?" said David Crone, one of Billy and Suzy's fringe friends. "Look Frenchie, the best minds of the school are at this table."

Your accent is terrible, thought Suzy.

I am fluent in any language on the planet, Fame thought, *but accents make no sense to me.*

"Weakness has nothing to do with intelligence," Billy explained to the rest of the table.

"Oui," said Fame. "A weak mind belongz to zee parson who is inzecure; who haz low zelf-ezteem."

"Insecure?" said Suzy. "Low self-esteem? You just described every kid in every high school everywhere."

"Eet doez not matt'r how smart zey are. Zey are vulnerable tu… tu…?"

"The Dark Side," said Billy to a collection of the biggest *Star Wars* fans in the city.

"Join me, Luke!" said three or four of them together.

"What iz zee differenze between a bullee and person zey are bullying? Zee bullee haz zee weak mind."

"Tell us something we don't know," said Suzy.

"Tell us something we can understand," said Crone about her accent.

"Zee bullee most often choozez victimz zat share traitz zey do not like within zemzelvez."

"So Stockwell beats up Billy because Stockwell is smart?" asked Crone.

"He iz smart enough to know zat Billee haz zomething he will never have."

"Yeah, brains."

"No. Friendz. Peaze of mind. 'Appiness. Billee haz ziz, he doez not, so he must destroy Billee. I feel zorry for bulleez zometimez. Zey are zad people."

This revelation brought a lull to the conversation, so

Fame went to stealth mode. *Of course, just because bullies are sad people doesn't mean you should stick around. You're not safe here.*

While Billy and Suzy contemplated that, and so many other things, everyone else in the school contemplated them. The silence was excruciating. Finally, Billy couldn't take it anymore.

"This is ridiculous." He got up and marched across the courtyard to the Coven's table. Suzy and Fame scrambled to catch-up, followed by their supporting Geeks. Behind them the rest of the student body.

Billy noticed the sound of a herd behind him, stopped and turned. Collectively everyone froze like a dangerous game of red light/green light. No one knew what Billy would do, but everyone expected something gossip-worthy.

He walked up to the Coven. "Linda, Sonni, Mary, Amy," he said with a nod to each of them, "I'm sorry about what happened on Friday. I didn't mean to cause the damage I did, and I'm glad no one got hurt. I hope we can forget the whole thing, and finish out the last two weeks of school like nothing happened."

The young women collectively paused. The crowd held their breath.

Careful, Billy. These girls are surrounded by dark consciousness. Your mind is too strong for the darkness to get at you directly, so they'll go through these girls. Don't be goaded.

Linda stood to speak. "You are such a child. Do you think we care about your 12-year-old sense of humor? Your cheap chemistry-set effects and your silly theatrics?"

"We don't," said Sonni.

"Not in the least," said Mary.

"We don't care about you at all, Billy Bobble," said Amy.

"What we do care about," Linda continued in what must have been a rehearsed speech, "is that you disrespected the Craft."

"And for that," said Sonni.

"You will pay," they all said together as they stood to face him as a unified front.

Linda stuck out her hand. "Give me the wand."

I don't mean to say I told you so, thought Fame, *but...*

"I don't have it," said Billy.

"Get it," said Mary.

"Get it now," said Sony.

"If you do," said Amy, and together they all finished her thought, "we'll make it worth your while."

"Yu du not know vhat you are mezzing vit."

"Fame!" said Billy.

"Zer are dark forzez yu know nozing about."

What are you doing!? You told me not to be baited.

They are being fed dark psychic energy from my world, thought Fame. *It's addictive and dangerous. If they think it is successful they'll never stop. They'll become a vehicle for your quantum enemies.*

What can I do? thought Billy.

Don't let them win.

Don't let them win, what? This showdown? She had to be kidding. Did she know who these girls were? "I... I..."

Linda took his stutter as a sign. "You've been cursed."

Mary said, "Give us the wand and we'll lift the curse."

Sony added, "We'll set you free."

Amy finished with, "just give us the stick."

"No… I…" Billy turned to Fame. "What do I do?"

Linda answered instead. "You give us the wand and beg for forgiveness."

Don't give into them, Billy, thought Fame. *If the girls feel their curse is working, they'll be puppets of dark consciousness forever. It will eat their souls.*

"…souls?"

"That's right, your soul—" said Sonni

"Is cursed," said Mary.

"Forever," said Amy.

"Unless," said Linda, "you give us the wand."

"No… I…" Billy was trying to think what to do. He was being humiliated and bullied. That was nothing new. Sure, this time it was being done by the forces of darkness from across the divide, who were using the minds of his peers as proxies—but still, it amounted to the same thing. Bullying and humiliation. How do you beat a bully? Think…

"I… I…" Got it. "I think we need another show of magic," he announced to the crowd. "What do you say, people?" They cheered, and Billy had his weapon. You fight humiliation like you do fire, turn it against itself.

"You do tricks, Billy," said Linda.

"That's not magic," said Sonni.

"Not *real* magic," said Mary.

Amy was left hanging. "…yeah."

"No, we're talking real magic. And if I was cursed…" He stood up on the picnic table to address the crowd. "I obviously couldn't perform any magic, could I?"

"No!" said the kids, ready for a show.

From his perch, Billy could see through the windows. A couple of vice principals were running down the hall to stop whatever was going on, so he said, "We'll have to make it quick." He offered his hand to, "Fame?"

She took it and joined him on top of the table.

"Have you all met our lovely French exchange student?" asked Billy. "Her name is Fame."

The girls politely applauded. The boys whistled and hollered, as Fame did make a unique, attractive, young French lady inside the heads of each of them.

"Bobble!" shouted one of the adults from across the courtyard. "Stop what you're doing right now!"

"I would, sir," Billy shouted back, "but then the Coven will think that you were part of their curse, and—I'm sorry girls—I can't let that happen."

Normally, Suzy would have tried to talk Billy out of such a display, but she was privy to Fame's side of the conversation. She had no love for the Coven, but she didn't want to see anyone hurt over this. And besides, as she looked up at her old geeky friend, watching him defy authority, manage an unruly crowd, and suavely escort his attractive assistant, Suzy got the feeling that Billy was… dare she think it? … cool.

"All right," he said, getting back to the show. "Without any smoke and mirrors. Without a curtain or a box to hide any tricks, and hopefully without any explosions…" The last bit was played for a laugh, which he got. "…I will turn this young girl into a cute little cat.

Very clever, thought Fame.

I bet Suzy is yelling at you to tell me to stop.

No. That is not what Suzy is thinking at all.

"Bobble!" The adults were pushing through the crowd. "One, two…"

"Au revoir," said Fame with a little wave.

"Three!" Billy snapped his fingers, and Fame turned into her cat form. The kids gasped. "Real magic! No curse." He looked down at Fame and snapped his fingers again. She took her human form once more, this time wearing a cheerleader's uniform.

The kids screamed like they were at a pep rally. The Coven looked defeated.

"Stop this! Stop this right now!" The vice principals had finally made it to the front of the mob.

How are those dark consciousnesses? Billy asked Fame.

Much better. The Coven have lost their false sense of power, and the laughter and entertainment seems to have chased the darkness away.

That's good, thought Billy, *'cause we're off to the principal's office.*

IV

"I don't recall seeing any paperwork on you, Miss…?"

"Eez only 'Fame,' sir," said Billy's familiar to Mr. Dillon.

She, Billy, and Suzy already sat through a lecture about stirring up trouble, and how, just because they are the heads of their class, it's no reason that they should, blah, blah, blah… which was the point where Mr. Dillon realized he'd never seen Fame before, and had no idea what her class ranking might be. He was perfectly willing to accept the French exchange student story, if he could just find her paperwork.

While he looked on his desk, the two human kids and one Quantum teenager were shocked to see another copy of Billy lean into existence behind the principal, as if poking his head around an invisible curtain in reality. This newer Billy held a finger up to his lips to tell himself and his friends to be quiet. He then showed them a file folder marked FAME TRANSFER PAPERS, pulled out a DVD of *Bill and Ted's Excellent Adventure,* and a piece of paper that read, DON'T FORGET TO WATCH THIS IN THE FUTURE. He put the file on Dillon's credenza, made a very strange air-guitar motion with his tongue hanging out, and leaned back out of their reality.

"I am shure zey are 'ere zomewhare," said Fame as her human friends stifled a laugh.

"This is not a laughing matter." Dillon's bark might have worked on other kids, but these knew that he had no bite for them. "I have recruiters from the best prep schools in the world coming to talk to you. Both of you. What will I say to them if you're suspended?"

Billy's mind started to spin. There are no coincidences. *Why would these recruiters suddenly decide to come check in on a couple of underage kids?* he thought.

"I'm sorry, sir, but what exactly did we do wrong?" Suzy might have missed her calling in biology. She'd make a great lawyer.

Good, Billy. You're starting to see how they work, thought Fame.

"Well… you were…" said Dillon. "You were… acting up."

"Acting up?" Suzy asked. Besides giving Dillon a way to let them off the hook, she was also running interference for the telepathic conversation flying around the room.

"Yes. And we can't have any of that."

They want to make sure I come back to school, thought Billy.

Possibly.

But why?

"No, of course not," said Suzy.

They control the Coven, and the Coven controls you.

That's crazy. Billy protested a smidge too much. *They don't control me.*

That's not what Suzy says.

But we won, right? The girls minds are free of influence, aren't they?

Yes, for now. But humiliation is not a good way to banish evil influences. Not for long.

Meanwhile, Suzy kept up the vocal discourse with Dillon. "I'm sure I speak for all of us when I say..." Her sincerity was inspired, "...we are terribly sorry for ... acting up ... and we will do our best not to ever do it again."

"Well." Dillon shifted in his chair a bit, not sure if he hadn't just been out played by the youngest students on campus. "I'm glad to hear it, and thank you for the apology."

"Is that all, sir?"

"No. It's not all." Dillon stood up to collect his thoughts. When he walked around his chair he saw the file on his credenza. "Ah, there's the paperwork, good. Good. Now, I'd like to see you two here tomorrow to meet with those recruiters I mentioned."

"Yes, sir," said Billy and Suzy together.

"And, Billy, if you could stop by Mrs. Dillon's desk, I believe she has questions about the database."

"Yes, sir."

Dillon didn't have to tell these kids twice. They were up and out the door in a heartbeat.

Things weren't so easy with Suzy's dad.

"What part of 'Top Secret' didn't you understand?"

Suzy heard an opening in her father's tirade and came to Billy's defense. "He didn't have a choice, Dad."

"There is *always* a choice, young lady." His voice shook their basement as much as the wand had, and that thought made Billy appreciate that Mr. Dillon must not have filled the General in all of the details. If he had, Quinofski would want to know how Billy did magic without his wand.

The upstart answer to that question lay on the sofa, kneading a pillow with her claws. *Suzy says you should tell him everything.*

No, thought Billy. *Merlin told **me** to think of something new, not anyone else.* While Fame relayed that to Suzy, Billy said aloud, "I'm sorry about today. This just… It's a lot of pressure."

Maybe it wasn't an accident that kids invented this thing, Billy thought. *Adults aren't so good with new ideas.*

Should I tell Suzy what you said?

Absolutely.

"Apology accepted," said the General, unaware of the weighty decisions being made around him. "I can't do a thing about the pressure except keep you busy. I need you two over at the base, if you're up for it."

"Of course," they both said.

"Good. We've got a war to stop."

"Yes, sir!"

Billy, wondered if they were talking about the same war.

Nineteen

Magic Lessons

On the morning of day two of Hocus Pocus, Billy had to brief the strike force on how to use a wand before heading off to school.

"I don't really know how it works," Billy said to the men once the General got things started. "I mean, I know that it uses an electromagnetic implosion field to disassociate the core introns' connection to Time and Space, which puts any matching coding DNA into the Quantum World where all moments in Time are connected to all places in Space. I know that in the Quantum World consciousness is everything. You think it, and it happens, which can be really freaky."

The soldiers all laughed about the possibilities of what they might think.

"Stow it," the General barked.

"Believe me," said Billy, "it's not funny. If you think the wrong thing, you could find yourself floating in the middle of non-existence with no way back to your previous reality, and there is nothing fun about that."

"I would love to have the luxury of time to study how this Quantum World works, but we have a mission here." Quinofski turned to Billy. "If you were one of these soldiers, how would you use the wand to get our people back?"

Billy had been thinking about this since he heard of the situation. He had more questions than answers. "Where exactly are they being held?"

"We don't know for sure."

"That's a problem," said Billy. "And even if you did know, and had an exact GPS location—that doesn't help in consciousness navigation."

"Consciousness Navigation?" asked a Lieutenant.

"Yeah, I made that up," said Billy, "but it makes sense, right? I mean, if you know the exact latitude and longitude of a place can you think of it? Can you get such a strong mental image of a bunch of numbers that you could get yourself there out of all the other possible places to go in the universe?"

The soldiers didn't have an answer. The physicists, who apparently couldn't proceed without Billy and so were eavesdropping, nodded like they understood, but Billy wasn't sure they did.

"Going into the quantum world that first time…" Billy stopped himself. He hadn't told anyone how horrible it had been, not even Suzy. He had to push the memory back or he wouldn't be able to continue.

The soldiers recognized Billy's body language: the look-away, the pursed lips, the eyes up to hold back tears. They all were combat veterans. They had seen and done things they didn't want to remember, and certainly didn't want to talk about. They gave their young comrade the silent respect he needed to collect himself.

Billy tried to go on. "It was… the worst thing…" but he wasn't ready. His gaze went to the floor.

"Hoo-ah," whispered one of the soldiers. "Hoo-ah," said the rest just as softly.

Billy sensed the energy in the room change. He raised his head and found a quiet, caring look of respect on the faces of the soldiers. He felt something with them he'd only ever experienced with Suzy before, a bond that he couldn't quite explain. With Suzy it came from so many shared experiences, but he had nothing in common with these battle-hardened men and women. They were tough. They had fought in wars. They had seen horrors that no human being should ever see.

Maybe they did have something in common.

Billy wiped away a tear, then continued. "I found my way back from nothingness by thinking about home. And when I could finally figure out how to let go of the button—or, even what a button was, or where my fingers were within the cosmos—that thought brought me, not home, but to a holding cell with Suzy."

The scientists sported looks that said they understood something Billy didn't, but they were wrong.

"You don't have to be a rocket psychiatrist to realize that I feel, deep in my heart, that hanging out with Suzy is more like home than hanging out with my hoarding mother and red-neck brother—but the point is, I was thinking about the literal definition of 'home,' but the Quantum World heard my feelings instead."

Billy felt the silent stares of his audience. He looked down at his shoes but stuck to the point. "Consciousness Navigation. It's not enough to think of the words. You have to know what the words mean to you."

General Quinofski brought the class to an end. "All right, ladies and gentlemen, it sounds like you've all got homework to do."

Billy interrupted with one more bit of advice. "Don't get lost in the quantum world. Don't let you mind wander. If you lose control of your thoughts, it gets really bad, really fast."

The General paused to make sure Billy was done. "Thank you, Billy." He then addressed the adults. "I want a wand strategy meeting at sixteen hundred hours when the kids are back from school."

The physicists rushed up to Billy like fans to a movie star. They had been working on his wand to make it more directional and were eager to test it. Billy had enough time before school started, so he went along.

They took him to an area outside, where they'd set up a target. It was a black-and-white cartoonish drawing of an obvious bad guy that needed dealing with, and looked like something they'd found in a 1970s FBI junk locker. Billy stared into the eyes of the cigar-chewing, beret-wearing, villain with the oversized Tommy gun pointing at him and he felt a pit grow in his stomach. Zapping this figure of a fellow human being into splinters was nothing like Merlin's new idea.

"All right Billy, here we go," said one of the scientists. He was as excited as a kid behind the scenes at a fireworks show. Around him the rest of the team gathered, just as eager.

Billy was led to a spot about twenty feet from the target. "Blow that bugger to hell," cried one of the soldiers.

It's not a weapon, thought Billy. *It's better than that.*

True, came a familiar voice from nowhere but inside his head, *but there is a weapon in the character's hand.* It was the Teacher. *And if you don't do something about that, he will certainly kill you.*

Knowing that the Teacher—Merlin—was looking after him gave Billy confidence.

Even King Arthur had a sword, huh? thought Billy.

Still. A sword wasn't much different from a wand as a weapon. It wasn't a new idea, but he didn't have the time to come up with that right now. He had to think of something quick. If he could pull the cartoon gun from the cartoon man's hands, then he would have neutralized the threat without too much violence. He concentrated on that, pointed his wand and fired.

Once again, Time slowed for Billy. The Wand Build Team had done a good job. Instead of an explosion of white condensate, he was looking down his wand at the energy as it raced toward the target—which was now alive and running right at him! Like the gnomes he'd seen in his backyard, this inanimate object now had a kind of life in it—and it wanted Billy dead. As the character serpentined toward Billy, the shot from his wand followed every move, bending and twisting. Finally, the energy caught up to the target at the very spot it had stood before the spell began.

On contact, Billy imagined the energy yanking the gun from the villain's hand.

In real time, Suzy and everyone else saw a jagged bolt of lightning flash from Billy's wand, hit the target and blow it to smoking bits in the blink of an eye.

Cheers from the crowd returned Billy to normal time. At his feet lay the shattered remains of what had been the gun portion of the drawing on the target. Twenty feet away was a ¾-inch piece of plywood with a hole blown out of it. Only Billy noticed that the hole was where the character's gun had been. He hoped that, had the person been real, he could have let go of before his arms ripped off.

"You should tell him," said Suzy.

You should also get your wand back. Fame was in her cat form. The three of them were supposed to be on their way to school, but hadn't left yet.

"Tell him what?" General Quinofski surprised them. They didn't know he was right inside the barracks they loitered in front of.

"Well, sir," said Billy. "I need to get my wand back."

"Have some pressing magic that needs doing?"

"Possibly, yeah."

"There's a lot you don't know, Dad." Suzy's outburst made Billy's full confession unavoidable.

"Okay. Why don't you two fill me in?"

As they went inside the General's onsite headquarters, Billy started a thought-versation. *Tell Suzy I'm not telling him about you, Fame.*

She asked 'why not?'

I don't know. Just a gut feeling.

"Have a seat, Billy, Suzy. That cat seems to have taken a liking to you both."

"Meow."

"She's definitely good to have around in these stressful times."

Quinofski smiled in that way Billy normally found annoying. "*How cute, the children are talking like grown-ups.*" He wasn't annoyed now, since he was the one smiling on the inside.

"So what is this I don't know?" asked Quinofski.

"Do you remember the other day when you said I looked tired and I said it was personal stuff?"

"Yes."

"Well, it was more than that." Billy started his story with the cleaning of his house and got into such detail that Suzy suggested he get to the point. Billy told him about the Teacher's second visit, and the gnomes, and his mother, and about how evil forces are after him, and the trap, and thinking of something new.

"If we hadn't had our little brunch the other day, I'd swear you were paranoid."

"But, Daddy! He's not. He needs his wand—"

Quinofski held up his hand to his daughter for patience. "I did have breakfast explode all over me and then removed completely. I'm a believer, honey, no worries there." He walked around to his desk and pressed a button on his phone. "Quinofski to all department heads. We need to be done with the prototype in the next ten minutes."

A chorus of complaints came up from his intercom speaker.

"We'll discuss details at this evening's meeting, but I need the object in my office ASAP."

That didn't stop the complaints, but pressing the drop button did. The General turned back to the kids. "The thing is, we haven't been able to replicate wands for our squad, so no one wants to give up the only one that works."

"They'd better." The voice came from behind Billy and Suzy, who turned to find the Teacher sitting in the plush couch in the conversation area of the large office. He still had the long white hair and flowing beard, but wore a three-piece wool suit, complete with a pocket watch, and reminded Billy of a picture he'd seen of George Bernard Shaw—though, for the life of him, he couldn't remember what Shaw was famous for. "That wand is like Excalibur. I think you'll have trouble making a copy."

"Uh. Hi," said Billy. He never expected his imaginary friend to show up in front of others.

The old man stood. "Introductions, please, Mr. Bobble."

Suzy and Billy showed their well-trained manners and stood as well. "Sure" said Billy, "Uh. General Quinofski, Suzy, this is, um... Merlin, or uh... Prometheus, or The Teacher."

"Suzy, it is an honor to meet you. I'm a big fan of your work."

Suzy blushed. "Thank you, sir. Billy's told us all about you."

"Well... all that he knows." The old man had a twinkle to his smile. "General, do you mind if I ask you a question?"

"By all means."

Billy was impressed by the General's acceptance of this strange man who appeared from nowhere.

"In this modern day and age, who is a soldier's true enemy?"

The General's answer came without a single pause for thought. "In a nuclear age, the true enemy is war itself."

"Ha! *Crimson Tide*," said The Teacher with the energy of a teenager. "One of the best submarine movies ever made."

"Billy," said the General, "this is a very wise man. It's hard to tell a classic before it has stood the test of time."

"We'll get along fine, General," said the Teacher. His tone made it sound like he was leaving.

"Is that all you came for?" asked Quinofski.

The old man lowered his head in deep contemplation, then popped up as if the answer had just come to him. "Yes. For now." With a smile, he left the way he came in, which is to say he disappeared.

"That was weird," said Suzy.

"Welcome to my world," said Billy.

Just then a soldier came in with a small shipping tube and handed it to the General. "Thank you, soldier. Dismissed." The young man left with a quick, curious glance toward the kids. The General gave Billy the package. "Here you go, son. If you wouldn't mind keeping that under wraps, I'd appreciate it."

"No worries, sir."

Under wraps, but at the ready, said Fame.

Twenty

Man-fume

"What now?" Billy and Suzy were summoned to the office before they could get to study hall and another run-in with the Witches of Winston High.

"Jinx!" said Suzy.

"I guess that means you'll be doing all of the talking?" Their version of jinx was that the other person couldn't talk until someone said their name; but neither one of them ever stuck to it.

"What do you think it's about?"

"No idea."

Before they even walked into the office, Billy had sniffed out the answer. Dr. Menaus, from Oakridge Academy. Billy would know that man-fume anywhere. Then he remembered what Dillon had told them on Monday.

Scouts from the best schools were coming to see them. Around here, that meant Oakridge.

"Billy, I'm so glad to be the one making this visit," said Dr. Menaus as soon as they stepped into the outer office. "And you must be Suzy Quinofski. I've heard a lot of good things about the daughter of the town's famous general."

"Thank you," said Suzy.

Billy once again found himself making introductions. "This is Dr. Menaus. He runs the physics department at Oakridge."

"Oh, so you're the one we have to thank for all the lab time," said Suzy.

Menaus put his finger to his lips. "Shhh. That's not official." He nodded toward his colleague like it was a big secret.

The colleague was an attractive woman of an age the kids couldn't determine, (i.e. as old as their parents). "I'm Dr. Hensen," she said, offering her hand to them both. "Dean of admissions."

"Wow, you have to have a doctorate just to run admissions?" asked Suzy.

"I'm afraid so."

"I think we're the ones who should be afraid."

"Nonsense, Billy," said Dr. Menaus. "We've been following you two for years."

Just then Mr. Dillon came out of his office to greet his guests. "I see you're all getting acquainted, that's good. Come in, let's have a chat."

It took a while for the seating to be sorted out and the niceties to get out of the way before Dr. Hensen got things started. "Billy, Suzy, we wanted to talk to you today about the possibility of coming to Oakridge next year. Now, before you say anything, I want you to know we're talking about full academic scholarships for both of you."

"You realize we nearly blew up the school the other day?" asked Suzy.

"As Mr. Dillon has explained to us, that was an unfortunate accident," said Dr. Menaus. "And, being a physics teacher, I know that explosions aren't always a bad thing."

He and Dillon laughed at this little witticism. Dr. Hensen did not. "We often find that advanced kids get bored in school and may express their frustration with delinquent acts."

"That must make Peter a genius," Billy said to Suzy. She giggled. No one else laughed, not even Mr. Dillon, who knew Peter well enough to get the joke.

Dr. Hensen pressed on. "Trust me, you wouldn't be the first kids we've let in with bad marks on their record."

She was nervous. All the adults were. Billy wasn't sure how he knew that. Maybe it was their laughs, or the forced smiles, but something was wrong about their behavior—and Billy was not paranoid. "I thought we were too young for Oakridge."

"Yes, well, fifteen is our minimum age for new students," said Dr. Hensen, "but—"

Dr. Menaus cut her off. "Billeeeee..." He spread out his hands in an "oh, come on!" gesture. "Since when has age been an issue with you?"

Billy noticed that he didn't get an answer to his question, but skipped it. "Shouldn't our parents be here?"

"Ah, yes," said Dr. Hensen again, and again Billy got the feeling she was nervous. "We normally do have this discussion with parents present, but, Billy... we've done our research. We know that your mother isn't in the best of health."

"She's in better shape than you know," said Billy. He wondered how many gnomes she would see manipulating the adults in this room.

"That's good to hear, Billy," said Dr. Hensen, though her tone suggested he was a naive child for thinking so. "We weren't aware of that when we made these plans. We thought it would be better to talk to the two of you together first, then we could talk to your parents, Suzy, and Billy, I guess we would discuss details with your brother?"

Billy got a chuckle out of that idea. "Yeah, you doctors can talk to Peter." He shifted in his chair to give him a chance to glance over to Suzy. Clearly, they both missed Fame right at that moment.

They left the meeting with brochures and paperwork to take home.

"Finally! I get to get out of this dump and into a real school," said Suzy.

"Yeah. Funny how they are willing to bend the rules just for us."

"You heard the man, Billy. People have been bending rules for us all our lives."

"Why do you think that is?"

"Duh, Billy, because we're insanely smart."

"Interesting choice of words."

The rest of the day, even lunch, went by with a great deal

of stress, stares, and behind-the-back whispering. In other words, pretty much like any other day in high school. When classes let out, a Humvee waited for Suzy and Billy in front of the school busses.

"I was kind of looking forward to our walk," said Suzy when she saw their car, driver, and her mother.

"Yeah, me too," said Billy.

"Come on, kids. Your father wants to show us something." Mrs. Q often used the phrase "your father" around the two of them, and every time Billy told himself that it didn't bother him.

Neither of the kids spoke of the depth of humiliation Mrs. Q hoisted upon them as they climbed into the vehicle. She obliviously carried on about what charity event she was supposed to be preparing for so the kids weren't able to get a word in about Oakridge before they found themselves back at Hocus Pocus central.

The three of them were shown into the General's office, where they joined two vaguely familiar-looking men. "This cat is becoming the team mascot," said the General.

Fame sat in the General's chair. *Just keeping an eye on things.*

"What's up?" thought Billy.

Not sure. It's all your-world type of stuff, though General Daddy did tell the cops that the wand works just like Suzy said it did.

Interesting...

The General shoed Fame out of the way. "Billy, you remember Detectives Danner and Reins?"

Billy recalled that they had been at his motel surrender.

"Yeah. Are we in trouble again?"

"Not that I'm aware of," said Danner.

The General explained, "Something our researchers noticed that I thought you should all see and consider."

He turned toward a flat screen TV on the wall and pressed a remote. The image was Suzy in the interrogation room.

"You recognize this, Suzy?"

"Yeah."

On screen, Mrs. Quinofski enters:

"Don't say anything. Your Dad's on his way, and I'm getting an attorney."

"They don't believe me, do they?"

"It doesn't matter what they believe, honey. It matters what they can prove. Wait here."

The two detectives gave Mrs. Quinofski a hard look, then a yeah-you-were-right shrug.

"Everything as it was so far?" the General asked his daughter.

He had his kind-but-serious tone going, so she said, "Yes, sir."

On screen, Suzy suddenly popped out of the picture, replaced by:

"Is that my ficus tree?"

"That's not right," said Billy.

"Yeah, Billy appeared. I told him what was going on, then he told me to think about my lab and we disappeared. I don't know how the tree got there."

"And the chair?" asked Danner.

Billy answered. "Yeah, I blocked the door with one of the chairs."

"And there was no explosion like we heard," said Reins.

"I'm going to run it again. Watch the time code," said the General Quinofski. Sure enough, the numbers go smoothly at first, then jump ahead. "Two minutes and ten seconds are missing."

A hush fell over the room and all eyes landed on Billy.

"Don't look at me! I didn't even know we were being recorded." *Fame? Any thoughts?*

Nothing relevant.

"Is this something your wand could do?" asked Danner.

"I thought we weren't supposed to talk about that," Billy said to Quinofski.

"Good answer," said the General. "These detectives are cleared. You can speak freely."

"Honestly, I don't know," said Billy. "I suppose it's possible, but if the wand works the way I think it does, I would have had to have thought of doing something like that, and I didn't."

"Could Suzy's thoughts have done it?" asked Danner.

Reins added, "You were quick to point out that you knew you were being recorded."

"That was hours before. Besides, I wanted you to see Billy's wand at work so I didn't seem so crazy."

"True," said Danner.

"Honey, what is this?" Mrs. Quinofski noticed the Oakridge material sticking out of her book bag.

"Oh, I was going to tell you, a couple of people from Oakridge Prep came to school today to offer Billy and I scholarships."

"Honey, that's amazing!" said Mrs. Quinofski

"Aren't you too young for them?" asked her father.

"Yeah, but Dr. Menaus knows Billy from way back, because he uses the lab up there, so they said they'd make an exception in our case."

"Wait." Reins thought he recognized the name. "Dr. Menaus. Is he a slick guy that smells like he crash-landed into a cologne factory?"

The kids both laughed. Suzy answered. "Yeah, that's him."

Reins raised an eyebrow to his partner, who clarified. "You spoke to Dr. Menaus today?"

"Yeah, we both did," said Billy.

"Just about your scholarships?"

"Yeah."

"He didn't mention anything else?"

"No. Should he have?"

Instead of answering the question, Danner and Reins stood. Danner did the talking. "General, how do we stand from a jurisdictional point of view on this?"

"If you think you can find out what happened—"

"Oh, we have a good idea," said Reins.

"It would be obstruction of justice if I ask you to bring evidence to me before your District Attorney…"

Reins shook his head in annoyance. "General, you might be glued to the rule book, but we're small town juvenile division detectives, we could give a flying—"

Danner cut him off. "You can't ask, but we can offer."

"They aren't telling us something about Dr. Menaus."

"You think?" Suzy told her mother that she and Billy would rather walk home. The kids didn't miss the isn't-that-cute look between mother and father. Fine, let them imagine what they will about puppy love and Suzy not wanting to be seen with her parents. The kids knew the real reason. They had to talk.

"The Teacher said there are no coincidences where we're concerned," said Billy. "So we invent a magic wand and all of a sudden Oakridge is ready to break their rules for us? The guy leading the charge then makes the cops arch and hiss like cats. No offense, Fame."

"None taken," she had changed to her human form as soon as they left the base. "Want me to follow the cops?"

"No. Dad'll fill me in at dinner."

Billy's stomach knotted a little. Nothing big. Nothing to complain about. It was a feeling he'd get from time-to-time; though, if he'd done a chart he'd realize the feeling came and went with General Quinofski's infrequent visits home.

"You want to join us?"

"What?"

"Dinner. My place," said Suzy.

"Oh. Yeah. But, I want to check in with Mom first."

That was a different response, but, "Sure, no problem. Fame? Uh... cat food?"

"Are you kidding? That stuff is nasty. Besides, I have to check in on things back home, too."

"Home?" asked Suzy. "You have a home?"

"Duh! What do think, that I just came into existence for your benefit?"

"I don't know. Maybe."

"Well, I didn't. I have a life in the quantum world, and I'd appreciate the evening off, if you don't mind."

Suzy noticed that Billy wasn't joining in on a conversation that he'd normally find fascinating. "What are you thinking?"

"That things are getting complicated."

Twenty-One

If Wishes Were Fishes

"Thank God you're here," said Peter the minute Billy walked in the door. "I was about to call 9-1-1."

"Billy, run!" his mother shouted. "They're after you! Run, Billy!"

"She's been like this for an hour," said Peter. "Forget her invisible friends, if she doesn't shut-up soon and take her meds, I'm the one she's going to have to worry about."

Billy ignored his brother. "Mom, is it just the gnomes?"

"Yes! They're everywhere. Hundreds of them."

"Mom, look at me," said Billy. He needed her to focus and she did. "The gnomes are just scouts. They can't hurt you, okay?"

"But they're everywhere."

"I know. I've seen them. You're not crazy. But the gnomes aren't a threat. In fact..." Billy took the shipping tube out of his back pocket. "I might be able to do something about them." He drew his wand from the tube.

Peter grinned. "That's a great idea. Do you think she'll buy it?"

Billy said in all seriousness, "She's not the one I'm worried about."

"What?"

"Give me a second." Billy had to think. Lesser beings from the quantum world had staked out his house and were terrorizing his mother. What could he do to make it better? The part of his brain that comes up with cartoony ideas as a way of breaking the ice chimed in, *an invisible force field would be cool.*

At first Billy dismissed this as latent childishness, but then he remembered—an atomic bomb is nothing in the quantum world compared to a little boy's nightmares. He let his thoughts run. An invisible force field that would only let in beings from his reality could work—but that would mean Fame and the Teacher would be locked out, too.

Okay. How about a password?

Sure, why not? But would there then have to be a guard? Who is going to check for the password?

The force field. If you think of the password, the force field lets you in.

How will a force field know if you thought of the right password?

Duh! It's a *magic* force field.

"It's worth a try," Billy finally said out loud. "Mom? Are the gnomes inside the house?"

"They're everywhere," she whispered.

"Okay." Billy stood and gathered his thoughts. "Banish gnomes," he said and activated the wand.

A white cloud of energy made the little men and women visible in Billy's slowed down magic-time. From this cloud, little lightning bolts whipped around the trailer, crackling, splintering, and snapping fleeing gnomes.

"Holy cow!" said Peter. "That was awesome."

Billy didn't think Peter could see the gnomes because he wasn't completely freaked out. Billy saw them running away with little burn marks on their butts, but he wasn't sure he'd gotten them all. "Mom, are they all gone?"

"Yes, but they'll be back. You can't keep them out."

"Wanna bet?" Billy raised his wand and shouted, "Invisible Force field!" When he pressed the button, a bubble of energy exploded from the tip, expanded out to the edge of their lot, then faded into nothingness.

Peter was less impressed this time. "'Invisible force field?' Really? You think she'll buy that?"

"It doesn't matter what she thinks."

"But still. 'Invisible Force Field?' Why don't you just say, 'Wonder Twins Unite?' It might be a little less geeky."

"Oh, the problem is it's not cool? Should I have said, '*Scutum absconditum*' instead?"

"Well that sounds a lot cooler. What is it?"

"Roughly, 'invisible force field' in Latin."

"You speak Latin?"

"*Nimirum, omnis homo eruditus linguam Latinam dicit*," said Billy, hoping it came out as "all educated people speak Latin." Then he got back to the matters at hand. "Mom, look outside what do you see?"

She went to a window and giggled. "Oh, are they mad. They can't get in."

"That's good, Mom. The gnomes can never get inside this house, okay?"

"Okay. Good job."

With the gnomes locked out, Billy tried an experiment. *Fame, could I bother you to come here for a second?*

Ouch! What the —?

Sorry. That's my new quantum force field. The password is "no gnomes is good gnomes."

Less than a second later, Fame-the-cat, jumped up on the couch. *You could have warned me.*

Had to test the password protection. Have you met my mom?

Not yet.

"Mom, I want you to meet my cat, Fame."

Mrs. Bobble startled at the sight of the cat at first, but then relaxed. "Oh, she's a good one."

"Yes, she is," said Billy. He made note of how his mother could tell the difference between good and evil quantum beings. He'd have to figure out how she did that. "Mom, this is a very good cat. You can talk to her. In fact, talking to her is just like talking to me."

"Pets make good friends, don't they?" she said. "It's good for a boy to have a good friend."

Meanwhile, Peter stepped behind his mother to see what he could out of the window. "I don't know what you did, but she believes it's working, so I'm all for it. Anything that keeps her from going crazy like that is fine by me."

"She's not crazy, Peter. Well, she is, but… It's hard to explain. Just know that everything she says is true. The gnomes are real. They can't hurt you, but they can make you hurt yourself, so listen to her."

Dinner was less dramatic. Compared to his family, Billy always felt like Suzy's was something out of an old black & white TV show, the picture-perfect American home. All they needed was a loveably clumsy dog, but Mrs. Q was allergic.

Suzy asked about the video and why the cops seemed so interested in Dr. Menaus.

Her mother answered before her father got to. "Speaking of Dr. Menaus... Billy, were your mother and brother excited to hear about the Oakridge offer?"

"Oh, uh... I forgot to tell them. We had other things to deal with."

Mrs. Quinofski's power to step around Billy's weightier issues in an effort to lighten his moods was well practiced. "Well, I'm excited for both of you. This is a fantastic opportunity. Not many kids from around here get to study at such a prestigious boarding school. Of course, you two will live at home, I hope."

"They call us 'townies,'" said Suzy. "It's not a term of endearment."

"Oh, I'm sure there'll be some hazing at first," said her mother, "but things'll settle out soon enough."

"General Quinofski," said Billy, "you were going to say something about the video and Dr. Menaus?"

"Yes. The detectives were very curious to know why Dr. Menaus didn't mention that he witnessed Suzy's interrogation."

"He did?" asked Suzy. "Mom! Why didn't you tell me? Who else was there? Principal Dillon? The whole school?"

"I'm sorry, honey, I didn't know anyone was there. I found out after your interview there was a psychiatrist—"

"A psychiatrist?! Mom!"

"Well, honey, from their perspective, you did try to blow up the school."

"It gets worse," said the General. "They think he might have witnessed Billy's magical appearance and erased that part of the tape."

"Did they arrest him?" asked Billy.

"No. They want to keep a close eye on him. See what he's up to."

"Do you think that's why we got invited to Oakridge? So he could get his hands on the wand?"

Quinofski thought about this for a second. "Yes and no. I've talked to the principal and many of the board members of Oakridge over the years, so I know that they've always had plans to make the offer. This timing might just be a strange coincidence."

"There are no coincidences," said Suzy.

"Probably not. I just hope we can keep the lid on our secret a little bit longer."

"You two should stay away from that man," said Mrs. Quinofski. "He gives me the creeps."

Billy didn't want to talk about school or himself, so he changed the subject. "Any luck with the wands?"

"Not a bit," said the General. "I think we're going to have to scrap the idea and go back to more conventional means of extraction."

"But you don't know where the prisoners are being held," said Suzy.

"Well, one plan might be to have Billy stay on the base to zap our wand warriors in and out of locations for recon."

"What if I zap them into a terrorist training camp or something?"

General had a gift for understatement. "That would be a bad thing."

The trap. These villains had a way of making life tough on a kid. "General Quinofski, do you remember when I asked you for military lessons?"

"Of course."

"Well, I have a question."

"I hope I have an answer."

"Why is there war?"

Suzy's father didn't move for an uncomfortably long time. When he did finally, he took his last bite of steak, chewed, swallowed, wiped his mouth with his napkin, and said, "You know, I'm a general in the most highly trained, most lethal military machine the world has ever seen. I also hold two doctorates, one in military history and one in military science, so I am among the few people alive best-qualified to give a well-informed, intelligent, first-person answer to your question." He took a sip from his coffee. "Do you think you're ready for the answer?"

"I'm not sure, but I'd like to try it."

"The answer is … no one knows."

Billy wasn't sure if he was supposed to respond to that, so he didn't.

"No one likes war, especially those who have had to fight in them, and yet there hasn't been a single generation of human beings that lived in a time when a war, or genocide, or some other horrific slaughter wasn't raging somewhere on the planet. Nearly every culture or political system has been to war at some point in their history. War is so prevalent in our species that a better question might be, 'why is there peace?' If we knew that, maybe we could create more of it."

"Do you think I could use my wand to save us from war?"

"If wishes were fishes, son."

Twenty-Two

The Bullies of Stoners' Row

Wednesday morning Billy noticed something different at school. It was subtle, but definitely different. First, the stares. Sure, kids had stared at him before. At the beginning of every year he and Suzy would get the "do they really belong here?" looks. Those faded with the changing leaves.

The past couple of days he noticed the "that's the kid who blew up the school" looks. These were quick glances out of the corner of the eye. The kids he had classes with didn't bother to stare, though they might point him out to other friends in the hall. This all seemed harmless to Billy. Kids being jerks. Typical. He knew from the way his mother watched TMZ that they wouldn't grow out of it. They would become adults being jerks. Such is life.

But that morning the stares were long and hard. No

one looked away. They were angry and they wanted Billy to know it.

"Fame, are you seeing what I'm seeing?" After spending yesterday spying on the wand build team, Fame returned to her French exchange student disguise to keep an eye on Billy.

Do you have your wand?

"It's in my jacket pocket."

Keep it close. Dark forces are gathering.

"Yeah, great. But what am I supposed to do with it?"

Protect yourself. Protect the wand.

Billy ran into Suzy on her way to study hall.

"What's going on?" she asked before he could.

"I don't know, but it's weird."

"Where's Fame?"

"She's snooping around to see what she can learn."

The second bell rang just as they scooted inside the classroom.

Ever since the first day of school, Billy would agonize over what he'd say to Linda and the coven the next day in study hall, the last few days more so than usual. As soon as he sat down, the four girls turned to stare at him with the angriest looks they could muster.

"I'm sorry about what happened the other day," said Billy. "I didn't want to turn it into a big show, but..." He acted like he suddenly decided to take a new train of thought, but he'd planned the pause. He couldn't tell them the whole truth. They'd only laugh, so he had to dance around it. "You said that I'd disrespected the craft, and before all of this stuff happened, I have to admit I had no respect for witchcraft, or prayer, or luck, or anything that relied on faith alone. In many ways, I still don't, but I've learned that the universe is more complicated than we have ever imagined. Life is more than what we know it to be. And thoughts—whether they come in the form of a spell, or a prayer, or a curse, or whatever—are real. Imagination is real. It creates cause and effect. Good thoughts, good effects. Bad thoughts... who knows what will happen?"

"You're babbling, Bobble," said Linda.

"Get to the point," said Mary.

"We haven't got all day," said Sonni.

"Yeah," said Lisa.

Billy wasn't holding up well, so Suzy came to his rescue. "He's just trying to say he's sorry."

"We don't care," said Linda.

"You two are leaving next year," said Mary.

"You're going to Oakridge. Everyone knows," said Sonni.

"Oakridge is gross," said Lisa.

So that's where the stares are coming from, thought Billy, before he realized Fame wasn't there to pass the message along.

"They're mad because we're going to Oakridge," said Suzy in the hall.

"I haven't even made up my mind about that yet."

"Come on, Bobble, you know we're going. We have to."

"I don't know anything anymore."

"*You* don't know anything?!" Suzy stopped her dash to class and grabbed him by the shoulders. "Who are you and what have you done with my friend, Billy?"

He shook her loose. "Come off it, Suz', you know what I mean. Dr. Menaus can't be trusted."

"Maybe, but the reputation of Oakridge Academy can."

They came to the point in the hall where they had to part ways toward their respective classes. "Can we talk about this later?" asked Billy.

"Can? No. We *will* talk about this sooner than later."

"Fine."

Suzy ducked into her AP biology class. Billy turned to go to computer science, but was waylaid by a wall of flesh.

"Bobble head. We need to talk." It was the offensive line of the football team. All juniors. All big. All mad.

"I'll pencil you in for lunch," said Billy. He tried to scoot around them, but had no luck. Before he knew what was happening, they had him by the arms, heading to the gym.

Every school has an area for illicit student activities. Billy was about to learn about "stoners' row," the area behind the gym where there were no security cameras, and no vice-principals bothered to patrol. Billy's face-to-face meeting with this patch of dirt was literal, as he ate a bit of it when his escorts threw him to the ground.

"Oakridge?" said Sean Villar. He played left tackle, the position that had an entire movie named after it. Rumor had it, Sean watched *The Blind Side* before every game.

"How are we supposed to pass our senior year if you're not here?" With his face in the dirt, Billy couldn't see for sure, but he thought that might be tight end, George Graves, a big shot at Winston High, but the word was he'd wash out in college. Billy knew he'd never made the all-academic team.

He tried to stand up. "Guys, listen—"

"No, you listen!" A punch to his stomach and a kick in the kidneys put Billy back on the ground. It also sent his wand tumbling out of his jacket pocket.

"What's this?"

Billy looked up to his horror. Scott Stockwell had his wand. "Scott... don't..."

"Don't what? Break your little toy?" He tried to snap the stick in half.

Fame! thought Billy.

Way ahead of you.

Stockwell tried to break the wand over his thigh.

Fame, who was nowhere to be seen, laughed inside Billy's head. *How long should I let him keep trying to break the unbreakable?*

But Scott answered that question for them. "So it won't break? Maybe we can play fetch." He flung the wand as far over the gym as he could.

Billy watched it sail away, then heard Fame behind him. *Billy, catch!* He turned just in time to snag his wand, as if Stockwell had thrown it around the world. The others were stunned for a second, which would have been the time for Billy to come up with some kind of impressive magic, but instead, he grinned at his attackers, thinking Fame's trick had been cool enough.

It wasn't. Sean clocked Billy square in the nose with a hard right. Blood shot out, but Billy hit the ground before the blood did. Involuntary tears filled his eyes. He was seeing double and everything was spinning. Another kick and Billy was sure he felt a rib or two crack.

This wasn't the run-of-the-mill bullying he'd expected. It was a full-on beating. Billy was in danger for his life, but the only magic he'd thought of was for a lesser occasion. Still, he conjured up his images, shouted, "*Crescite menda!*" and fired.

The cold white energy splashed out of the wand like electric milk from a fountain. It washed over each of Billy's attackers. They stopped beating him and he heard laughter.

"Dude, your ears!"

"Dude, your zits!"

Billy looked up to see Sean's ears, which always stuck out more than most kids, were three times as big as they used to be and well past his shoulders. George Graves had never had a stellar complexion, but now every inch of exposed skin oozed with oily, pus-popping zits. Judging from the wet spots all over his shirt, the problem extended over the skin Billy couldn't see.

"It's Dumbo and pus-face," said someone Billy couldn't see, but he didn't have to. The once tough-guy's voice was now a high soprano. When Billy rolled over he saw Stockwell was about two feet tall and dressed like one of the Lollipop Guild from the Wizard of Oz.

Billy's idea for a spell had worked. *Crescite menda*, Expand Faults. He figured everyone is self-conscious about something, so he reached into the universe where thought is king, found his enemy's insecurities, and then ... inflated them a bit.

Okay, more than a bit.

Each kid wanted to laugh at his friends, and at the same time run, hide, and cry about his own condition. It didn't take long before they realized who had done this to them.

Billy was quicker this time. "*Scutum absconditum.*" He pressed the button on his wand, and George's furious punches landed on something as hard as concrete that he couldn't see at all. Sean cracked a toe the same way. Stockwell simply cried himself out of the picture. Two others Billy didn't know were long gone. Sean and George ran off as well.

Safe inside his invisible shield, Billy pinched his nose to stop the bleeding, which sent new shards of pain through his face. When he cried out, his ribs sent him reeling. He would never get to his feet, so he thought of the school nurse's office and fired his wand.

Nothing happened.

"Fame! What's wrong? Why can't I transport?"

Her muffled voice came into his head, *My guess is because you're inside a force field.*

"Oh, yeah."

And I wouldn't go to the school nurse. Too much explaining to do.

"Right. I'll go to the base. Tell Suzy, would you?"

Of course.

Billy activated his wand. "*Ablega scutum absconditum,*" banish force field. He then thought of the nice soft chairs in General Quinofski's office. When he activated the wand again, he popped out of existence.

Twenty-Three

Fishin' in the Quantum World

It takes a lot to startle a battle-tested army General, but Billy managed it easily. First by suddenly appearing in the overstuffed chair by the coffee table in his office, and second by his obvious injuries.

"Lieutenant!" shouted the General. "I need a medic in here on the double."

"What day is it?" asked Billy through his bloody nose, cracked ribs, and General Quinofski's handkerchief, which was now pressed against his face. "What time is it? How long was I out?"

"It's Wednesday, 11:50," said the General. His cell phone rang. "It's Suzy." He answered it.

"I must be getting better at this," said Billy to no one in particular.

"Yes, honey he's right here with a bloody nose and some bruises, but I think he'll be fine."

The beating must have given Billy an adrenaline rush, because he was feeling cavalier enough to find cell phones obsolete. He thought of Suzy standing before him and activated the wand.

Wham!

With a flash and a bang, Suzy appeared, still talking to her father on the phone.

"I am definitely getting better at this," said Billy.

Suzy took her magical abduction from school in stride. "Billy! Are you okay?"

"Been better. How about you?"

"Don't be stupid. What happened?"

"Seems like a bunch of juniors didn't like the idea of Mr. Homework going off to Oakridge."

A team of medics rushed into the office, but General Quinofski held up a finger. "One second." He knelt down next to Billy. "What did they do when you disappeared?"

"Nothing. They were running away by then."

Suzy was astonished. "Running away? Billy, no one runs away from you."

He held up his wand. "They do now."

The General glanced back to see if the medics were eavesdropping. They weren't. "Billy, what did you do?"

"It was bad. Trust me, I've been beaten up a lot. This was different." As if to prove him right, Billy's rib shortened his breath.

"I'm not saying you did anything wrong, son. I just need to know what kind of containment we're dealing with. What did you do?"

"I played You're Not So Perfect," said Billy through the pain.

Suzy explained. "It's a game we used to play when kids bugged us. Walking home, we'd talk about how they shouldn't pick on us because they weren't perfect either. You know, 'Scott Stockwell's not so perfect, he looks like a giant munchkin,' or something like that."

"You should see him now," said Billy. He laughed, which was a painful mistake. When he recovered he said, "I used the wand to find out what they didn't like about themselves and blew it all out of proportion."

Satisfied, the General waved the medics over. "Take good care of him." Then to Billy, "You're right. You are getting better at that thing."

Billy found himself sitting in the middle of a white nothingness. Not even a shadow smudged the perfect lack of anything.

And then, sitting next to him on what turned out to be a small pier that started in nothing, and stretched out over more nothing, was the Teacher. He was fishing. His pole was Billy's wand.

"I'm dreaming, huh?"

"What gave it away?" asked the old man.

"What are you fishing for?"

"A new idea."

"Is that the same one I'm supposed to come up with?"

"I hope not."

"I don't like talking in dreams," said Billy. "It's very ... broken."

"These are your dreams?" The Teacher pulled in his line. He'd caught nothing. In fact, he didn't even have bait on his hook. "You need to get better dreams." He cast his line out again. "Do you remember when I told you that 'they' were a part of us?"

"Yeah."

"I meant that literally."

Billy thought he was going to explain more, but got only silence. "What are you saying?"

"Some say my enigmatic teaching style is for the student's sake, and it is, but not for the reasons they think. I can't know too much about what you're going to do, Billy, because if I know it, they know it." He pulled his line out of the water again. Still nothing. He sighed. "If wishes were fishes."

"What?"

He tossed the line back in the water. "When you first saw me, you thought I looked familiar, yes?"

"Yes."

"That's because we met before."

"We did? Where?"

"Where you are now," said Merlin.

"Where am I?"

"You're in the hospital."

It took Billy a second to realize Suzy had answered his last question. He opened his eyes. Sure enough, he was in a private room in the hospital surrounded by the Quinofskis and Bobbles.

"One of those bastards almost punctured your lung," said Suzy.

"Don't worry, kid," said his brother. "I'm on it."

"Peter, no. Don't. I don't want to start a war over this." Billy closed his eyes again.

"That's right, Billy," said his mother. "Those boys didn't know what they were doing." Her voice was clear, not crazy at all.

Billy opened his eyes to find that he and his mother were the only people inside his white-nothing world. "I'm dreaming again."

"Of course you are, honey."

"What did you mean, they didn't know what they were doing?"

"They were compelled, Billy."

"By the gnomes?"

"Don't be silly, dear. Gnomes don't have that kind of power." She looked around the completely empty space they occupied. It was like being inside a light bulb that was on. "This place is filthy, Billy. You sleep now while I straighten up a bit."

Though he knew he was already asleep, Billy found that he couldn't keep his eyes open. He slipped into a world without dreams.

"Billy? Do you have a minute?"

The voice was vaguely familiar but sounded like a whisper that came from miles away.

"I have all the minutes," said Billy. His mouth was dry as cotton and his eyes didn't want to open, but he felt he wasn't alone, so he forced himself awake.

Detectives Danner and Reins joined the crowd in his room. The former said, "Sorry, to wake you, but... we need to show you something." He gestured toward the door, which Reins opened.

In stepped Billy's attackers, still sporting magical makeovers. Their heads were down, in a hat-in-hand humility that Billy felt might have had a good dose of fear mixed in.

"Dude!" There was a hint of respect in Peter's voice. "Did you do that?"

"I had to do something, didn't I?"

"I guess you don't need me to whale on these guys, then huh? You did a better job than my friends and I ever could."

The fact that these guys let Peter talk that way without mouthing off spoke volumes. They had been humiliated into submission.

Danner asked, "Billy, are these the boys who beat you up?"

"I... uh. I'd rather not say, officially."

"Bobble, tell them."

Billy couldn't see who said that until he looked over the foot of his bed. Scott Stockwell was too short to be seen from where Billy sat. "Oh, hi Scott. I didn't see you come in."

"If it'll make this go away, please tell them."

That was the General's cue. "Boys." Billy marveled at how he could command silent respect with a single word. That was some powerful magic. "What Billy did to you is part of a top secret military experiment he has been working on for me. That makes him an employee of the United States Army. Being Townies, I'm sure you know what that means. Military justice. That right to a phone call you might be expecting? You don't get one. An attorney? Nope. Your butts are mine."

Sean was the only one brave enough to speak up. "Sir, please. We're sorry. We don't even know why we did it. One minute everything was fine, the next, we're dragging Billy out of school."

"You're apologizing to the wrong man," said the General. He led Sean's gaze to Billy.

Sean got it. "Billy, little dude. What can I say? I'm sorry, man. We all are, right?"

The other kids nodded.

"I don't know if you still get to call me 'little dude.'" Billy looked over his bed and noticed Scott wouldn't make eye contact, so he asked, "Scott?"

"You know, up until yesterday morning, I thought of you kind of as a friend in a way. When I heard you were going to Oakridge, I lost it, you know? I got so angry, I didn't know what was happening."

"You should work on your anger issues," Billy said.

"Yeah, I'll do that, as soon as..." he indicated his tiny body.

Billy grinned a bit. He looked over at Suzy for the first time and together they nearly broke out laughing.

"It's not funny!" said Sean. Obviously, his big ears

could pick up their repressed snickers.

"No, it's not funny," said Billy. "It's not funny now. It wasn't funny when you laughed at me and Suzy all our lives. You made fun of us because of the way we talk. You teased us for being so smart, or the way we dress, or how we act. Do you know why you did that?"

No one wanted to offer an answer, or even raise their gaze above floor-level.

"You did it because you're afraid of what I turned you into. Dumbo-ears Sean. Zit-head George. Stocky Stockwell. I found your insecurities and blew them out of proportion the same way you have been doing to kids like me and Suzy every day. How do you like it?"

When no one said anything, General Quinofski did. "The man asked you a question."

They all mumbled variations of "we don't like it at all."

Quinofski turned to Billy. "Son, do you mind if I offer a deal?"

"Be my guest."

"Boys, if you make two promises, then I'll say you're square with the US Army. You might still have criminal charges and school discipline to face, but I won't throw you into a deep dark hole. Sound good?"

"Yes, sir," they said in unison.

"All right, here are the promises: First, you can never say a word about what you've seen of Billy's wand."

"Don't worry sir," said George. He'd been quiet up to this point, but Billy caught a tinge of hope in his voice. "We don't want to talk about his wand. Not ever. Not after what he did."

"Fine," said the General. "Next, not only do you

have to promise to never bully anyone again, you promise that if you see, hear, or smell bullying you put a stop to it. Understand?"

"Yes, sir."

Stockwell followed up with, "Sir? Can Billy change us back?"

"Why don't you ask him?"

Finally, all the boys lifted their heads to make eye contact with Billy.

"Make 'em beg," said Suzy.

"Forget that, make 'em give you money," said Peter.

"The thing is," said Billy. He let the moment drag out. "I'm not sure I can change them back."

Panic takes on many forms: heart palpitations, tears, shortness of breath, vertigo. The boys put on a grand display of all these symptoms and more.

"Guys, relax," said Billy. "I said I wasn't sure, not that I absolutely couldn't."

Billy.

Billy and Suzy eyes snapped toward each other.

Fame? Thought Billy. *Where are you?*

Uh... you could say I'm working from home. There's something here you should see.

Okay... how do I get there?

I'm not sure, but you could try activating your wand while thinking about coming to see me.

Right here, in front of everyone?

Don't worry. They'll never know you're gone, and if I'm right, we can put these kids back to normal.

Okay.

He looked at the kids he once feared, who now cowered

before him. "You guys better hope I don't screw this up."

Billy raised his wand. "Do you wish this had never happened to you? Do you wish you were exactly the same now as you were before you beat me up?"

"Yes!"

"Wish hard!" He pointed his wand, thought *Find Fame*, and fired.

"Fame?"

"I'm here."

"Where?"

"Wherever you want me to be."

"I thought I was supposed to come to where you are."

"Yes, but I can't be anywhere until you imagine it."

"What?"

"You have to imagine what you want the Quantum World to be before it can be anything."

"But I don't want to imagine it, I want it to be what it really is."

"Billy, it's a world of pure imagination."

Suddenly, Fame popped into existence in front of Billy, but she didn't look at all like herself. She wore a purple crushed velvet tailcoat and a clashing top hat over her impossibly curly hair. She stood in the middle of Billy's hospital room, where everything that was white was now made of vanilla icing, and all of the people were made of chocolate, like the Easter Bunnies his mom would bring home from work the day after the holiday.

"Holy cow, you're Willy Wonka," said Billy.

"Really? Which one? Johnny Depp or Gene Wilder?" She crossed her fingers, closed her eyes and wished, "Please say Gene Wilder. Please say Gene Wilder... Gene Wilder, Gene Wilder."

"I don't even know who that is."

Fame stopped wishing. "Then what made you think of Willy Wonka?"

"I don't know. Didn't he say that his factory was a world of pure imagination?"

"Ah! Gene Wilder! Excellent!"

"What is going on?"

She sang, "Come with me, and you'll see..." then jumped for joy. "Ha! I love it!" She landed next to the boys who attacked Billy. They didn't notice her, probably because they were chocolate. "Can you see the difference between this part of them," she knocked on Sean's chest, solid dark chocolate, "and this part?" She tapped his magically enhanced ears. They sounded hollow, and looked to be made of cheaper milk chocolate.

And then everything was gone.

Fame cried out. "Billy! What happened?"

"The Quantum Universe is not Willy Wonka's Chocolate Factory!"

"How do you know?"

"Because it isn't."

"It was a second ago," said Fame.

"Then why isn't it now?" said—or thought—Billy. He wasn't sure which.

"Because you lost faith."

"Lost faith? Faith in what?"

"In your own imagination."

Billy was on the edge of his temper, and the universe reflected his mood. Impossible swirls of everything, reduced to grains of sand, blew around them. Billy and Fame were simultaneously a part of the swirl and their usual selves, which just made Billy more confused. "Physics is not imaginary!"

"Oh, no?" said Fame. "What is the observer effect, then?"

The particles of everything in the universe instantly stopped swirling, froze for a second like cartoon characters in mid-air, then ran away to hide behind each other.

"The observer effect states that the act of observing a particle changes its properties."

"That's what you humans think, but in fact, the particle doesn't exist until you decide there should be one to observe."

"Really?" Billy considered this for a second... *It could be true.* He'd have to work out the math, but that didn't mean... "Just because a particle isn't there until we think it might be there, doesn't mean that when it appears it's a crumb from the floor of Willy Wonk's Chocolate Factory."

"There are no crumbs on the floor of my factory!"

"You're not Willy Wonka."

"You're no fun." Billy sensed his somewhat imaginary friend sigh. "Let's try this a different way," she said. "Tell me what you see."

"I don't even know how to open my eyes."

"They are open."

"Then I don't know how to tell you what I see. I—"

She cut him off. "Don't try. Close your eyes."

Billy concentrated with all of his might. "Are they

closed?"

"Doesn't matter, as long as you think they are."

"This place if friggin' weird."

Fame ignored the dis on her digs. "I want you to think in very simple thoughts about how you might see ... the most important particles in the hospital room. Not everything, just the simplest way you might see ... you know, matter-energy, energy-matter, blah-blah-blah."

"Blah-blah-blah?"

"Well, I don't want to make things too complicated in your head, just keep it simple. If you try to see everything you won't see anything at all."

Billy got the idea. "Maybe I shouldn't see anything. Start from nothing and build up."

"There is no nothing here."

"Yeah, well, there is in my head."

"Fine. Give it a try."

Billy thought of darkness and the wild, impossible universe faded to black. "Okay, that's good, it's dark now." He then thought about the simplest of images, coloring book drawings. Slowly, white outlines of the hospital room and all the people in it became clear. "Okay, I'm starting to see the room."

"Can you see the boys?"

"Yeah."

"Do you notice anything about them that's different from the others?"

"Not really. Everything is just, sort of, a cartoon outline of reality."

"Think about a little more detail."

Billy got a mental image of turning up the detail on

the picture, like with a TV. Soon he could see what Fame was talking about. "The parts of them that I put on with magic look different from the rest of them, and Scott looks like he's been stuffed into a trash bag or something."

"Exactly," said Fame.

"Why is that?"

"No idea, but I'm guessing it's like replacement car parts. They might look and act like the original stuff, but something about them just isn't right."

"What do you know about cars?"

"Whatever you know about cars."

"That's not much." Then Billy remembered a conversation he'd had with Peter a while back about original parts vs. knockoffs. Peter's garage began to impose on the hospital room.

"Billy, you're drifting. In the world of imagination, if your mind wonders, you go with it."

"Right, okay." He concentrated and the room became more... normal? No, but more like it was without the garage. "Matter-to-energy and back," he said to Fame. "I bet that, since it took billions of years to turn energy into the matter that makes up our bodies, and I made the same conversion in less than a second, that..." Billy started to lose his vision. The universe turned back into the indescribable everything. "What happened?"

"You're thinking too much. Normally, that's a good thing, but you're so fixated on what is real. You have to crawl before you can run."

Billy cleared his head and got back to the simple black and white version of things. "Okay, I can see again." In looking around the room he noticed something else.

Mentally, he turned up the detail of his image a little bit more.

Brightly colored mist surrounded each person in the room. Everyone had their own color, that not only surrounded them, but reached out to wrap around the others. "What is that colored mist?"

"Thoughts," said Fame.

"But they're all intertwined."

"Well, yeah. If you think about someone, your thoughts go out to them. Haven't you heard that expression?"

"Yeah, but I didn't know it was true!" Billy saw that most of the thoughts from the others wrapped around him, though, everyone had rope-like thoughts that went out into space. Between him and Suzy the thoughts were so woven together that he couldn't tell where they started or ended.

His mind began to race. A new idea was forming, which turned his vision back into everything. Mentally, he held onto the new idea, but tucked it away for later. His vision returned to something comprehendible, and he got back to the task at hand. "What do I do about these guys?"

"Your improvements on their looks are fragile. I'm betting that if you touch them with your wand, they'll disappear."

"I can't even open my eyes, how am I supposed to—"

"Just think about it. Simply."

Billy concentrated on the simplicity of holding his wand and moving his arm over to the boys, and it happened. He then thought about lightly touching them with the wand, and he did. His changes to their appearances puffed around them like a cloud of dust. Scott broke out of his little body and grew to full-size. "Cool," Billy said. "Now let go of the button on your wand."

There was no big explosion, just the crackling of energy shooting from the stick. When the foggy smoke cleared, the boys stood as normal as they were before—or, at least as close to normal as they were. Without a mirror in the room, they had to check each other to confirm that they were no longer freaks. Eventually, they thought it might be a good idea to thank Billy.

"Get out of here," he told them.

They scrambled out as fast as they could.

Billy ignored the pain in his ribs, sat up and said, "General. I think I know how to get your people home."

Twenty-Four

Hurry Up and Wait

"Get me McCrackin on a secure line," the General said into his cell phone.

Billy and the rest of the entourage hurried to keep up with the General as he stormed down the hospital halls. Billy pulled his jeans on under his hospital gown as he went. Biting down on his T-shirt helped him hide the pain of his broken body. He'd convinced everyone that he'd made his injuries magically disappear, but he hadn't. He just didn't want the world to fall apart because he had a bloody nose and wheezy chest.

He put his T-shirt on over the gown to hide his bruises. "Who's McCrackin?" he asked Suzy.

"White House Press Secretary."

"Pat," said the General, still on the phone. "That package we've been trying to keep under wraps? ... Well, heads up. It's about to be Christmas." He snapped his phone shut. "Billy, Suzy."

"Yes, sir," said Suzy.

Billy fell behind while pulling the gown out from under his shirt, but ran forward. "Here, sir."

Suzy noticed the strain in his voice. "Billy, you're still hurt," she whispered.

"Hush. I'm fine."

"Despite your friends' promises, I think our little secret is about to become public knowledge, or a national rumor. Either way, spotlights are sure to follow, so Billy, what's your idea?"

"The families, sir."

"Families?"

"Of the captured soldiers. Their wishes to see their loved ones again will be so strong that we don't need to know where the prisoners are being held. I can find them in the Quantum World and bring them home."

Without breaking stride, the General dismissed the kids with, "Good plan." Back into his phone he said, "Lieutenant, you still there? Good. Get me the President."

They passed an intersection in the hall that Billy found familiar. Looking to the right he saw the locked doors to the psych ward. He stopped to put on his shoes. The rest of his group flew past him toward the elevator.

Billy tied his shoes, but didn't take his eyes off the windows in the doors to the area where his mother had been held. In one, Billy recognized the hyperactive patient. He wasn't tall enough to look out, so Billy only got glimpses of him as he jumped up to see what was happening.

Framed in the other, was the old patient who had talked to him before. Billy froze. That old man was his old man, Prometheus, Merlin, The Teacher, but the smile on his face was not a friendly one.

From the hospital, Peter took his mom home. Mrs. Quinofski took Suzy and Billy to the Quinofski residence where they were to wait for the General to call them once he'd collected all the interested parties. "This is a classic military situation, kids," he told them. "Hurry up and wait. It might be a long one."

They didn't mind. Since the explosion at school, the two of them hadn't had a lot of time together to do nothing—which is often when so much in life gets done. After chocolate pop tarts with peanut butter and a couple of reruns of *The Big Bang Theory*, Suzy asked, "Billy? If our thoughts link to people, have you thought about, maybe, using that to find your dad?"

Billy's answer was immediate. "Nope."

"Why not?"

"Because I don't care."

"Billy!"

"Suzy!" His tone was serious enough to stop her protests. "I'm 12 years old. I've spent all of those years convincing myself that I don't care. That I don't want to know anything about my dad. And you know what? It's worked. I'm convinced. Okay?"

"Okay." Suzy got the feeling that the elephant in the room she'd awakened, stretched, yawned, and curled back into his comfortable spot on Billy's chest. The subject was dropped.

She picked up a new one. "Do you think we're walking into the trap?"

"No. I think Oakridge is the trap."

"What?"

"Think about it, Suzy. Dr. Menaus spooked the police, then he showed up to offer us a scholarship. And Merlin said I'd knowingly walk into the trap."

"You're knowingly going to walk into Dad's operation."

"Maybe so, and maybe it is the trap, but The Teacher told me to think of something new. I think I have."

A lull passed through the conversation, which Suzy chased away. "Oakridge, huh?"

"I think so."

"But the dark quantum whatever-they-ares have a good foothold at Winston High. They tried to use the Coven, and they definitely used the guys who beat you up."

"Exactly. If you want someone to run into a trap, what do you do?"

Suzy got it. "Chase them." She shifted in her seat and her head. "But... How can a prep school be a trap? Why would they want you there?"

"How many high level politicians and business people went to Oakridge?"

"I don't know. Some."

"If you include other prep schools, and the big universities they feed into?"

"Okay, a lot. Big deal."

"If you want to control a population, control their education."

"What is that? Like, from *The Art of War*, or something?"

"No, I just made it up. Kind of cool, though, huh?"

"Does that mean you're not going to take the scholarship?"

"I don't know. I'm still thinking about it. What about you?"

"Mom and Dad would kill me if I didn't."

The thought of school without each other sank the spirits of both kids. Suddenly, they didn't know where to look. They had nothing to say. Everything they did felt awkward. All conversation stopped. A movie, dinner, a couple of video games later and the subject was wordlessly put away for another time. After dessert and laughing over stupid imitations of their teachers, they were comfortable again and soon out cold on in front of the TV.

An unknown number of hours later, Fame jumped on the couch. *Wake up, you two. The show's about to begin.*

Twenty-Five

The Big Show

"Show" was the right word for it. The first act was a new ring of security around project Hocus Pocus. Eerie butterflies filled Billy's stomach as he, Suzy, and her mom neared a checkpoint with metal detectors staffed by soldiers he'd never seen before. "Do you know these guys?" he asked Suzy.

"They're Secret Service. Whenever the President visits, some of them dress as army soldiers."

"The President is here?"

"That would be my guess."

"No pressure, huh?" Billy remembered what Suzy's dad first told him about his wand. In a world with magic, how could they protect the President? The beeping of a metal detector scared the thought out of his head.

"Step this way, please," said the Secret Service officer dressed as an Army sergeant. She waved a handheld detector over Billy and got a signal from his jacket pocket. "Could you empty your pocket, please?"

"It's okay," said Mrs. Quinofski. "He's—"

"Ma'am," said the officer with force. "I don't care who he is. He has to empty his pockets."

"It's okay, Mrs. Q," said Billy. "It's just a little embarrassing," he told the officer, as he took out his wand. "Your detector caught the battery in the handle." He took it out to show her.

"My kid has one of those. I didn't know they came with batteries."

"This one's new," said Billy. "It lights up." He put the battery back, made little a wish, and pressed the button. The wand's tip glowed white, revealing suppressed snickers from the two Quinofskis.

"Oh, like in the movie."

"Yeah." Billy pretended to defend himself from his giggling companions. "What? It's dark on my walk home."

"Go ahead," said the officer.

They walked away from the checkpoint like kids who'd just pulled a prank.

"That saved us a lot of explaining," said Mrs. Quinofski.

"Yeah," said Billy. "And I just slipped the most dangerous weapon on the planet past the planet's highest security."

The closer they got to the Hocus Pocus project area, the more child-like Mrs. Quinofski became. After a few more security clearances—which all took the wand to be a novelty—she finally busted out. "Isn't this exciting? Meeting the President."

"We've met the President before, Mom."

"That was the other President, not *this* one."

Suzy rolled her eyes. As a general's wife, Mrs. Quinofskis had to stay politically neutral in public, but anyone who brought up the subject with her would soon know whom she favored.

"Billy," she asked, "You've never met the President. Aren't you excited?"

"More worried about how I'll do."

"Oh, of course. I'm sure you'll do fine."

"And I've met Merlin. The President is a bit of a step down after him."

The building they were led to had been set up as a theatre of sorts. In the audience were the wand-build scientists and the special ops team. The high profile guest and his entourage sat in the first row.

General Quinofski waved Billy and Suzy up to the front of the room where he stood before almost fifty civilians who Billy figured were the family members of the captured soldiers. "Mr. President, may I present my daughter Suzy and her friend, Billy Bobble."

Billy marveled at the awe-inspiring charisma of the man he'd seen so many times on TV. Think what you will about politics, there is no escaping the charm of anyone who holds the office.

"I've heard a lot about you, Suzy," said the President. "You've got one proud father."

"Thank you, sir." She curtseyed. Yes, army boots, attitude, and all, Suzy broke under the pressure of social graces and bent her knee for the President of the United States.

"Billy, General Quinofski tells me you might have made me the *second* most powerful man on the planet."

"Ah... I serve at the pleasure of the President, sir. That means you're still number one."

The great man gave the great boy a great smile. "Well spoken."

"Thank you, sir."

The President reached into his jacket pocket. "I'm told, you might also need this." He pulled out a double-A battery. The build team and soldiers chuckled politely.

Billy took it, even though he'd checked the battery before they left. "Thank you, sir."

"The President is here," said the General, "because we think our secret will be out soon, and he wants to see it in action first hand."

"I hope it works the way I want it to," said Billy.

The President pointed to the people behind Billy. "So do they. So do we all."

"Then we'd best get on with it, son." The General swept his hand toward center stage, indicating where Billy should stand.

Billy didn't move. "Right." He shifted his focus from the families and the audience and back again. He shuffled his feet a bit, then asked, "Have they been told what's happening?"

The General was left with his hand hanging out like no one would return his high five. It didn't seem to faze him. "They know what you know."

"Good. Okay, um..." Billy took the wand from his

coat pocket, slowly made his way to center stage and faced the families. "I feel like a conductor."

A nervous laugh floated through the room.

Billy cleared his throat and tried to ignore how dry his mouth had become. "I need you all to think real hard about... whoever it is you're related to that's captured overseas, okay?" He raised his wand.

"What should we think about them?" asked a man who must have been a father of one of the soldiers.

Now Billy's hand was left hanging. He wasn't ready for that question. He didn't know the answer. "Uh..." He lowered his arms. The expectant eyes that looked to him for help were red and swollen with tears. From the looks of their tissues, they'd been that way for a while. "It doesn't really matter," he said, and raised his hands again to add a flourish to his magic.

The people stirred in their seats. Billy felt the hope they'd had in him fade.

The father put their thoughts into words. "How can it not matter?"

Billy dropped his arms again with a sigh that could have been taken as a condescending tone. "In the Quantum World," he started, but he felt the crowd slipping further away. "Thoughts are real. They have energy, and..." Billy had lost them. He didn't know much about public speaking, but school reports had taught him when no one was listening, because they hardly ever did. He looked back to Suzy and her father for help.

Suzy stepped up beside him. "We need you to make a wish, okay? We need you to wish really hard that the person you're thinking of could be standing in front of you right now? Okay?"

That settled the crowd. Billy silently mouthed, "Thank you."

Suzy winked, then added one more instruction for the families. "We just need you to love them."

Billy saw the hope rush back into their eyes. "Thanks," he said to Suzy.

"Any time."

She went to sit back down, but Billy took her hand. "Stay?"

"Sure."

He wasn't sure why he'd asked her to do that. He wasn't going to take her into the Quantum World, but he liked the idea of having her around. He let go of her hand, concentrated, raised his wand, said, "*Consectatio desidero*," and pressed the button.

"Suzy says your Latin has gotten better."

Fame, dressed in her Willy Wonka outfit, stood in the middle of everything that ever was or will be in the universe. Her presence gave Billy comfort. "Yeah, weird, huh? 'Follow the wishes' is definitely cooler in Latin."

"She says you even got the *insectatio / consectatio* right and wants to know when you've had time to study."

"I haven't. That's what's weird. "He shook off that thought and concentrated on his new surroundings. All of everything threatened to boggle his mind, so he turned down the volume in his head. The universe faded to black. Only Fame remained unchanged, but it wasn't like she was standing in front of him—more as if she was inside his head, and he was nowhere at all.

He slowly turned up his internal Quantum Reality Dial. Like in the hospital, the people appeared as if from a mist until they became white line drawings of themselves. Billy got the idea that everything in his world had become a clean, black, chalkboard with people drawn on it.

And then came the rainbows of color.

"Check out the President," said Fame.

He was surrounded by a cloud of pastels. Sparks flew from his head and popped like 4th of July fireworks. "Man's got a lot on his mind."

Out of the darkness that encompassed the room, billions of bright strings arched over the crowd to wrap the President in a web of thought.

"And practically everyone alive has a thought about him," said Fame. "Careful of the dark colors, they come from bad places."

"Got it." Billy didn't want to think about bad things at the moment. In fact, he didn't want to think about much at all. His mission was too important to have the universe get crazy on him.

Where the President's thoughts were chaotic, the family members' were clear as a bell. Beautiful, shiny bright streams of consciousness rose from each of them, twisted together over their heads and flew off into the distance. "If wishes were fishes," said Billy.

And suddenly they were. The rope-like thoughts became streams of consciousness from which the wish-fish jumped. In their scales, Billy could see video-like images of kids playing, weddings, family reunions, and a million other remembrances or hopes for what might be. But Billy couldn't linger on them. Instead, he tried to grab the rope-like thoughts.

They dissolved in his hands. He couldn't get a grip. "What are you trying to do?" asked Fame.

"I was going to grab the thoughts and pull the people they are connected to across the Quantum World, to here."

"They aren't ropes anymore," said Fame, "they're rivers."

"I know that! What do I do about it?"

"Think them back into ropes."

But the more Billy tried to do that, the more they turned into rivers, and the more fishes of wishes flopped out of them. "It's not working!"

"You're letting your thoughts get away from you."

"How do I get them back?"

Red sheet lighting filled the Quantum World. Billy knew what that was.

"Don't get scared, Billy."

A wind picked up. "Too late."

The memory of his first disappearance broke free from whatever lockbox Billy tried to keep it in. Then, there was no Teacher. No Fame. No Suzy. His life was as empty as the universe he'd banished himself to. He had cried out for his brother, his mother, and even the father he'd never known. His only answer was a kind of horror that stopped him from breathing and turned his nothing universe into a nightmare that he didn't think he could survive. He had banished himself to nowhere, and it wasn't a lot different than his life. He remembered seeing Suzy's face for the last time before he pressed the button.

It might even have been the reason he'd wanted to disappear so badly. Tears. That's how bad his life had gotten. Tears from Suzy. Then, in the nothingness, he didn't even have that. He was in a place where there was nothing, including a desire to live.

He survived the horror then, but he knew there was no guarantee he'd live through it a second time.

Fame echoed the advice he'd given Suzy her first time. "It gets bad when you're scared." The wind became like a tornado.

"I know!" shouted Billy. He could sense it was getting worse. He felt a primal fear in his stomach. The kind of terror he must have felt as a kid, when monsters lurked under his bed and no one in his family would answer his cries.

The wind carried the not-so-distant bloodcurdling roar from such a monster, or such a kid.

"Billy!"

"How do I stop it?" He had to shout over the storm that now engulfed everything.

"The river is nothing but thoughts." Fame was shouting, too. "Good thoughts. You don't have to be afraid."

"That's not what I'm afraid of," said Billy. The unseen monster growled just outside of his sight.

"That... whatever it is," said Fame, "is from your imagination. Don't let your fears get the best of you."

"That's not what I'm afraid of, either." With that realization, Billy knew what he had to do. He dove into the outgoing river.

"What have you done?"

Fame's voice barely cut through the memories that enveloped Billy as he flew at the speed of thought through the flow. The memories were not his own. They belonged to the soldiers' loved ones. First days of school. Tears of joy. Laughter. Fights. Proms. Hilariously ruined Thanksgiving dinners. Births, deaths, funerals, and weddings. Billy learned everything about every soldier he was about to save as he sped around the world.

"Billy!" Fame's insistence took his focus. "What have you done?"

"It's not the thoughts I'm afraid of."

"Obviously!"

"I'm afraid of failure." Billy expected the admission to turn the quantum world into another nightmarish storm, but instead, the stream of consciousness that carried him seemed to slow to a leisurely pace. As if to say, "take a moment to figure this out. It's important."

"I couldn't go back to face all of those families, or the President, or the General, or Suzy as a failure. I couldn't let people down like that."

"I know," said Fame, and Billy knew it to be true.

"Do you think I willingly walked into a trap?" he asked.

"Not at all," said Fame, "but you might have jumped into one."

"Guess we'll find out, huh?"

Before Fame could say, "Guess so," the thoughts came to a swirling end at some other point in the Quantum World. Billy felt curiosity's tug. Part of him wanted to take his finger off the wand's button to see where he was for real, but he didn't dare.

Darkness dominated the whirlpools of color. He

concentrated on his level of awareness to show him an outline of the people around him.

On one side of what seemed like a room, a group of people huddled. The brightly colored rivers of thoughts surrounded them, as did another group of people. These held guns, which appeared as glowing red shapes, as if they'd just come from a blacksmith's fire. The outlines of these people were not as bright as the others, and the colors that flowed from them were dark.

Before Billy knew what was happening, black jets of smoke came out of the river to choke the men with guns. "Billy, that's death," said Fame.

"What?"

"The black smoke is death. The families want the other side dead, and your connection to the Quantum World could make their thoughts strong enough to do it."

"No," thought Billy. "That's not what this is about." He shouted out as if the families were just in the next room. The red lighting and violent winds returned. Billy raised his voice to cut through it all. "We have magic! We don't need revenge."

But nothing stopped the black smoke from surrounding the captors. Billy's actions began to flow from pure, hopeful, instinct. He snapped his wand around like it was the handle of a bullwhip, and suddenly it was. Strands of pure glowing white crackled with energy. He used the whip to ensnare everyone in the room. When he had them tied together, he jumped into the outgoing flow of thought. The current pulled Billy and everyone else into the river—where memories and death entwined equally. Before he knew which would win the day, Billy and his haul were back where Billy had started.

He let go of the button on his wand.

The concussive force of all those people popping into the airspace rocked the building. Cheers erupted before things stopped shaking. The freed prisoners were stunned when they found themselves in bear hugs from frightened but ecstatic loved ones.

In the midst of all this joy, Billy noticed men on the ground not moving. They weren't American soldiers. They were dressed in native clothes, carried Russian weapons, and were quite dead. "What happened?"

No one heard Billy's question. They were too overjoyed, too caught up in congratulating him to notice his distress.

"What happened here?"

He looked at the families. Tears were everywhere, but one woman's were not of joy. She stood alone, calling, "Mark! Where are you, Mark?"

Suzy, who had been hugging Billy, followed his stare. "What happened?"

"Nothing good."

A couple of the returned soldiers near the crying young woman noticed her. One took her by the hands, locked eyes and simply shook his head.

She collapsed. The soldier eased her to the floor. Her wails silenced the room. When she could finally speak; "Where is he?"

Everyone looked at their shoes, then glanced up at

Billy. He didn't know, so he said nothing.

"Where is his body?"

Death disconnects our two worlds, Billy. Fame, in cat form, curled around his feet. *Her wish couldn't bring him back.*

"Ma'am," said Billy as carefully as possible. "The magic can't work on the dead."

She pointed at the brown-skinned bodies lying on the floor. "What about **them**?"

An authoritative voice arched in from the back of the room. "They were alive when Billy brought them here." The Teacher. "Your wishes killed them." He was dressed like Obi-Wan Kenobi, though Billy remembered what Fame told him—each person will see a Quantum Being in their own personal way.

"My wish?" she cried. "I wished for my husband to be with me, alive."

"And if he wasn't alive?" asked the Teacher.

Billy watched her features change from sorrow to a cold, dangerous anger as she looked down on the dead men at her feet. "Then I wanted to kill the men who did it."

"Your wish..." the Teacher said to her, then indicated Billy, "...was his command."

"So what's wrong with that?" asked a burly family member. "I wanted them dead, just for taking my son." The other family members seemed to agree. The burly father put his hand on Billy's shoulder. "You did good, son. These bastards deserved to die."

Billy's skin went cold. He looked down at the dead

men and felt horrible responsibility. He stepped out from under the burly man's praise and held out his wand to the Teacher. "Can I...? Is there anything I can do?"

"I don't know how your wand works," said the old man, "but I know about death. These people are disconnected from both of our worlds, and not even a wish can bring them back."

Billy felt sick. He was sick of the wand. He was sick of not being paranoid. He was sick of gnomes and explosions and crazy people and war and traps and being beaten up. He wished it would all go away. He wished he'd never made a magic wand. He wished he could stop being a wizard and go back to just being a geek. He wished his wand would go away forever.

So he threw it as hard as he could.

The instant it left his hand, Billy knew he'd made a mistake. He'd walked into the trap. He'd done exactly what they wanted him to do. His wand flew across the room but never hit the wall. It disappeared.

Fame, what happened?

No answer.

"Teacher?"

No answer.

Teacher? Fame? Merlin? Prometheus?

There was no answer and something inside Billy knew there never would be. He had wished that he'd never even made a wand, and his wish had come...

But wait.

If he'd never made a wand, then he wouldn't be standing in that room, next to the President, with all those soldiers and dead men.

"I had a wand, right?" he asked Suzy.

"Yeah, and you just threw it into oblivion."

Horror emptied out his gut. The most powerful weapon in the universe, gone.

"What have I done?"

Twenty-Six

After Math

Everyone was understanding, or at least they told Billy they were. "We understand, Billy..."

But they couldn't possibly. They didn't have enough information to know what Billy did. His wand was unprotected in the Quantum World, exactly where it shouldn't be.

"Fame will guard it," said Suzy.

"Yeah." That was the first thing that made sense to him. Fame would guard it, but who would guard her? And if "they" are a part of "us," like the Teacher told him in his dream, then Fame having the wand was the same as the other side having it.

The returned soldiers were whisked away for debriefing. The dead were quickly covered. Debates sprang up about if they should be handed over to the city coroner's office for autopsy or not. Billy noticed no one talked about notifying their families.

The President stepped away from the circle of congratulants to tell Billy he'd done a great service to the country, humanity, etc. etc. He put his hand on Billy's shoulder in a clear signal that the boy should walk with him. Suzy and her father joined, while the families applauded the exit.

Once outside, they had as much privacy as one could expect under the circumstance. "I hear you two have been offered scholarships to Oakridge Academy."

The kids stole a surprised glance. "Word travels fast," said Billy.

"Half my cabinet including my Chief of Staff are alumni, so I got an earful when they heard I was canceling meetings to come here. From what they tell me, their time at Oakridge laid the foundation for all they've achieved since then."

"I think I've already achieved more than my fair share," said Billy.

"But think how much further you could go with the right education and support?"

"Don't worry, Mr. President," said Suzy. "We'll get him there."

"You'd better, young lady, or I'll have hell to pay back at the White House." The President then shook General Quinofski's hand. "Good job, General. I'd salute, but I'm a civilian."

"I appreciate the respect, sir."

"With those troops home, we can all sleep a little easier tonight."

"Yes, sir, Mr. President." Billy realized that was the first time he'd heard Suzy's dad speak in his talking-to-a-superior voice. He sounded a little bit like he was talking to Mrs. Quinofski.

As the Washington crew climbed onto their helicopter, Suzy said to Billy, "Walk you home?"

"Absolutely."

"What I don't get," said Billy as soon as they were out of everyone's earshot, "is why I can't talk to Fame or the Teacher."

"I don't understand why Fame doesn't return the wand."

"That's easy," said Billy. "She returned it when Scott threw it away, but that was different. This time I wished it away."

"So wish it back."

"How? I don't have a wand to make a wish with."

"Well, then," said Suzy with the fresh determination that a new plan always brings, "we'll have to make another one."

Discussion Questions

1. Can you relate to these characters? Do you have a Billy and Suzy in your school, office, family? What traits in Billy and Suzy do you see in yourself?

2. Why do you think Billy is so driven to make a magic wand?

3. Why does Suzy help him?

4. Billy and Suzy were both bullied in lower grades. How did they handle it? Have you been bullied before? How did you handle it?

5. What would you do if you had a magic wand?

6. How does your answer to question number five reflect on your character?

7. Suzy says the magical place she and Billy travel through is the wardrobe from *The Lion, The Witch and the Wardrobe*, and Billy briefly turns it into *Willy Wonka and the Chocolate Factory*. Did you notice other allusions to famous children's literature or movies that Billy might not have noticed?

8. The Teacher—aka Prometheus, aka Merlin, etc.— says "I have been the wise old father-teacher since

the first poor human wondered who his or her father might be." How many historical, fictional, or religious characters can you name that are very old men with long white hair and beards? How many of them carried a wooden staff or wand?

9. Do you think Suzy and Billy will become a couple, or are they one already and don't know it yet?

10. Billy asks "why is there war?" Why do you think humans have wars? Do you think some of the reasons are shown in this story?

11. Billy's Mom says that the gnomes make people do bad things. Have you ever felt "influenced" to do something you knew you shouldn't do? Did you do it, or did you fight off the urge?

12. What do you think Dr. Menaus is up to?

13. Will Billy and Suzy go to Oakridge or stay at Winston High?

14. How might their new wand be different from the old one?

15. What will the world be like once everyone knows magic is possible?

16. Do you think magic would make the world better, or worse?

Acknowledgements

It takes a village to raise a novel.

The mayor of this village is Matt Sinclair, the founder, editor, publisher, and Chief Elephant Officer of Elephant's Bookshelf Press. He and his company are a gift to the literary world. I foresee a future when Elephant's Bookshelf Press is held in the same esteem as Sun Records, Sundance Film Festival, or any other fertile ground for the discovery and growth of independent artists.

Many of the citizens of this village are from Agent-Query Connect, an online forum dedicated to authors helping authors find their way through the publishing business. So many people there helped me that I can't possibly name them all. I have only actually met a few of them, but they are all near and dear to me. Thank you all.

Matt secured a book design from R.C. Lewis before her novel, *Stitching Snow*, made it big. Mindy McGinnis has always been around to answer questions, despite being busy with *Not A Drop to Drink* and *In A Handful of Dust*. Cat Woods kept me from head-hopping early on, for which I am grateful. Look for her the anthology she edited, *Tales from the Bully Box*, also from Elephant's Bookshelf Press, and next year Cat's debut novel, *Abigail Bindle and the Slambook Scam*, also from Elephant's Bookshelf.

Kirbi Fagan is the artist in residence of this village. She's responsible for the wonderfully colorful artwork and her agent, Jodell Sadler, is responsible for making that possible. Charlee Hoffman took Kirbi's art to design the beautiful cover. I also need to thank proofreader Mary Serbe for her sharp eyes.

Virginie Aris corrected my French. As for the Latin, I owe a huge debt to filmmaker, actor, and Latin professor Miles Doleac. If you're looking for an excellent narrative film set among the egos of the university system, check out his movie, *The Historian*.

Speaking of movies, I need to thank everyone at Dances With Films festival, especially Leslee Scallon and Michael Trent, for putting up with my endless chatter about Billy and Suzy.

On the promotion side, Candace Robinson has been fantastic managing my blog tours and reviews, and Tessa Elwood built my website.

I want to give a shout out to Matt's wife, Maureen Sinclair. Thank you for loaning him to Billy and Suzy.

Barbara Short gets all my thanks and love for heading up of our little family all these years while I've been playing with my imaginary friends. She is the magic in my life.

R.S. Mellette, originally from Winston-Salem, N.C., now lives in Sherman Oaks, California, where he slaves away at turning his imaginary friends into real people. While working on *Xena: Warrior Princess*, he created and wrote *The Xena Scrolls* for Universal's New Media department. When an episode aired based on his characters, it became the first intellectual property to move from the Internet to television. R.S. works and blogs for the film festival Dances With Films and is founding member of the blog From The Write Angle.

When not writing, he spends time keeping the peace between his two cats and the family German Shepherd.

Coming in 2015

Billy Bobble and the Witch Hunt

Made in the USA
Charleston, SC
28 April 2016